The patter of onrushing feet brought Davy around in a blur. As fast as he was, he was not quite quick enough. He caught a glimpse of a tall Indian and tried to bring his rifle to bear, but the warrior was on him in a long bound. A bony shoulder rammed into his chest, bowling him over.

Somehow Davy held on to his rifle. Rolling when he landed, he shoved into a crouch and leveled his rifle. A flashing war club slammed against the barrel, swatting the gun from his grasp. He ducked under a blow that would have flattened him like a board, and clawed for a pistol.

Suddenly iron arms encircled Davy from behind. He was yanked to his feet, and the man holding him barked instructions in an unfamiliar tongue.

The warrior armed with the war club raised it to strike.

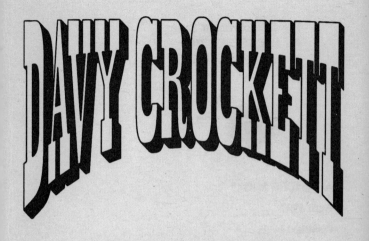

BLOOD HUNT

David Thompson

LEISURE BOOKS   ▙   **NEW YORK CITY**

To Judy, Joshua, and Shane

A LEISURE BOOK®

April 1997

Published by

Dorchester Publishing Co., Inc.
276 Fifth Avenue
New York, NY 10001

BLOOD HUNT

Chapter One

The wolves just kept coming.

Flavius Harris had a kink in his neck from twisting so often to keep track of the pack. "Damn it to blue blazes!" the stout Tennessean swore. "Why do those varmints keep following us? It ain't natural."

Seated astride a fine sorrel a few yards ahead, Davy Crockett turned his piercing blue eyes on the gray specters flitting through the shadowy woods behind them. "I don't rightly know what they're up to," he admitted.

And that worried the husky Irishman. A lifetime spent in the wilderness had made him familiar with the ways of all its many creatures. For a wolf pack to dog the heels of two riders for over an hour was so unusual, it was downright spooky.

"Maybe we should shoot one of the critters," Flavius suggested, nervously fingering his Kentucky rifle. "It might scare off the rest."

7

"It also might rile them enough to attack us," Davy said. "No, we don't fire unless they close in." His gaze rose to the mackerel sky. In the west a bloodred sun hovered above the distant horizon. Soon that fiery orb would sink and twilight would descend. Twilight, when wolves went on the prowl for food. Had these gotten an early start?

Flavius kneed his bay so it would go a bit faster. "If it ain't one thing, it's another," he groused. Ever since his friend had talked him into going on a "little gallivant," weeks ago, they had been through one harrowing ordeal after another.

Flavius couldn't blame Davy, though. No one had forced him to tag along. The prospect of getting away from his wife for a spell had been so tantalizing that he had leaped at the chance without a second thought.

More was the pity, Flavius mused. If he had known their gallivant would take them clear to the Great Lakes, or that they would tangle with hostile tribes that made the Creeks from back home seem tame by comparison, he would have wished Crockett well and stayed with Matilda. Being nagged to death beat being shot at all hollow.

The forest thinned. Davy spied a meadow ahead, dominated by a low grassy knoll in the center. It was a good spot to make a stand, if need be. Pointing, he said, "We'll stop yonder for the night."

"With these shaggy devils so blamed close?" Flavius squawked. He'd rather put their horses to a gallop and leave the wolves in the dust.

This wasn't the first time the pair had run into them. The remote regions they were exploring were rife with wildlife. Bears, deer, coyotes, rabbits, you name it, Flavius had seen more than he ever saw in Tennessee.

Davy made for the crest of the knoll. Sliding down, he looped the reins around his left wrist as a precaution, in case the pack attacked and spooked their mounts.

The wolves, though, halted at the edge of the trees, strung out in a long line. Some sat on their haunches and stared, their tongues lolling. Others paced restlessly. At their center was an enormous male with a silver-tipped coat. The end of his left ear was missing.

"The leader," Flavius commented.

Since the pack had yet to prove hostile, Davy proposed, "You fetch some firewood while I guard the horses."

To bring back wood meant venturing into the forest, a prospect that froze the blood in Flavius's veins. "I'm the one who should keep watch," he countered.

"Why you?" Davy asked.

Flavius racked his brain for a valid excuse. "Remember that bad tumble I took when that low limb clipped me? My shoulder is still awful sore."

Davy did indeed recollect the mishap. His companion had dozed off in the saddle and been unhorsed when a branch caught him across the chest. "That was nine or ten days ago," he noted.

"So?" Flavius moved his left shoulder up and down, then winced. "Can I help it if I'm a slow healer?"

Hiding a grin, Davy dismounted and struck off to the east. The wolves were glued to his every step. When he was halfway to the pines, several padded around the perimeter of the meadow to intercept him.

Davy was not overly worried. In addition to his rifle, he had a pair of flintlock pistols wedged under his wide leather belt, a butcher knife in a sheath on

David Thompson

his left hip, and a tomahawk on the right. He could hold his own against almost anything.

Plenty of dead, fallen limbs littered the carpet of pine needles. Davy kept one eye on the lupine predators as he gathered a sizable pile. Five of the beasts regarded him with interest but did not press close.

It occurred to Davy that they were more curious than threatening. Maybe Flavius and he were the first white men the pack had come across. Wild creatures who had never been hunted or trapped often displayed no fear of man.

Soon Davy had collected enough firewood. Bending at the knees, he was looping his left arm over the stack when one of the wolves—the huge one with the bit ear—ambled toward him. Immediately Davy brought up Liz, as he called his rifle in honor of his second wife, Elizabeth.

The wolf did not display the slightest trace of belligerence or fright. Limping ever so slightly, it approached to within six feet, then stopped.

Tense moments dragged by. Davy was ready to shoot if the beast so much as curled a lip, but the wolf simply stood there. "Well?" he prompted. "I don't have all day. Either put up or light a shuck."

Sometimes the mere sound of a human voice was enough to cause wild animals to flee. Not this one. The wolf sat and lifted its right forepaw as a hound trained to shake hands might do.

"Well, coon my dogs!" Davy exclaimed in amazement. "Don't this beat all." Unsure of exactly what the wolf had in mind, he did nothing.

A low whine escaped the animal. Cocking its head, the wolf wagged its paw.

"What do you want?" Davy wondered aloud. It was preposterous to think that the beast really wanted to shake. Could it be a ruse to distract him while the

10

rest pounced? Apparently not, because none of the others had moved.

Whining more loudly, the wolf narrowed the gap between them by half. Again it sat. Again it lifted the same paw and looked at him expectantly.

"What in tarnation?" Davy said. Slowly lowering his rifle, he cautiously leaned forward. Instead of snapping at him, the wolf extended the paw a little farther. Confounded, he studied it, and at first made no sense of the animal's peculiar behavior. Not until he bent lower and spied pus dripping from under the creature's foot did he comprehend.

"I'll be damned," Davy could not help saying. Gingerly, he reached out and lightly clasped the leg. Gently raising the paw high enough to see it clearly, he confirmed his hunch. Something was embedded deep in the callused pad.

As incredible as it seemed, the wolf apparently wanted Davy to remove the object. But how could that be? Davy had never heard tell of a wolf begging for help from a human before. Was it possible the animal had been in contact with people sometime in the past? Perhaps when it was a cub?

Another whine, punctuated by a rumbling rasp, ended Davy's speculation. Taking a gamble, he set Liz at his feet. The wolf offered no protest as he examined the wound. He wiped the pus on his sleeve and pried at the hole with a fingernail. Wary of causing pain that might provoke an attack, he peeled the pad back until he spotted the blunt end of a buried thorn.

"This is going to hurt some," Davy told the animal. Making no sudden moves, he drew his knife. A slanting sunbeam shone on the smooth steel.

Davy hefted the blade a few times, battling doubt. Removing the thorn was bound to hurt. What if the wolf reacted in the wrong manner? What if it sprang at his throat? The others would be on him before he could rise. He'd be torn to pieces.

The big wolf fidgeted.

"I must be shy a few marbles," Davy scolded himself, and applied the tip of the blade to the opening. As delicately as a sawbones doing surgery, he worked at the hole, inserting the knife far enough to hook the thorn.

Not once did the wolf growl or whimper. It sat rock-still, like a statue carved from solid granite.

Blood seeped from under the thorn as Davy attempted to ease the barb out—which was easier contemplated than done. He had to press harder than he liked, and move the thorn from side to side to loosen it.

Keenly aware of the wolf's fierce gaze fixed on him, Davy picked and prodded and wriggled and poked until the thorn jutted from the slit. With his free hand he plucked it loose and showed it to his patient.

"See? Here's the culprit."

The wolf sniffed once, then rose. Without another sound or a backward glance, it turned and loped off, the rest of the ghostly forms trailing. In moments they were swallowed by the lengthening shadows.

"You're welcome," Davy said softly, stupefied by the turn of events. No one back home would ever believe him should he relate the tale. They'd jest that he had guzzled one horn of liquor too many.

Tossing the thorn aside, Davy wiped his fingers on the pine needles. The incident was just the sort of thing that put zest into a gent's life. New people, new places, new sights—they were a heady tonic, part of the reason he was afflicted with incurable wanderlust.

Filling his arms with firewood, Davy retrieved Liz and started toward the meadow.

Blood Hunt

On top of the mound, Flavius Harris paced while gnawing his lower lip. The sun had dipped partway from sight. His friend had been gone much too long.

Afraid that Davy had been brought down before he could get off a shot, Flavius debated going into the woods after him. The wolves were bound to—

Flavius blinked. Was his mind playing tricks on him? Or was the pack truly gone? He scanned the tree line and did not discover a single wolf.

Frantic, now, that his friend was being feasted on by the four-legged fiends, Flavius cupped his mouth and hollered, "Crockett! Where are you?"

Davy chuckled as he strode into the open. "Right here, Ma," he quipped. He'd never met anyone who worried as much as Flavius. It was a minor miracle the man didn't have ulcers.

"Where'd the pack get to?"

"Shucks. I didn't think to ask. Want me to call them back?" Davy answered, and chuckled when his fellow Tennessean cussed a blue streak. "Now, now," he said. "What would Matilda say if she heard that outburst?"

Flavius frowned at the reminder. "She'd want to wash out my mouth with soap." His beloved was a devoted churchgoing woman who could no more abide foul language than she could taking the Lord's name in vain. He had to curb his tongue around her or suffer her wrath.

Davy kindled the fire at the base of the knoll on the southeast side. There they were sheltered from the northwest wind, which blew gusty and chill at night. Flavius tethered their horses, then deposited their saddles and blankets in the ring of firelight.

"What do you aim to do about supper?"

It was a good question. They were about out of

13

jerky and pemmican. "I'll see what I can rustle up," Davy said. Holding Liz in the crook of an elbow, he drifted westward. As the better hunter and better shot, filling their bellies was usually his job.

Creeping darkness claimed the woodland. Davy kept his eyes peeled for squirrels and rabbits and such, but had no luck. The wolves had scared all the smaller creatures into hiding. He was about to give up when the snap of a twig to the north rooted him in place.

Something was out there. Something big. Davy gauged its size by the crack, for only a heavy animal could make that loud a noise. He hoped it was a deer. The thought of fresh roasted venison made his mouth water. And whatever was left over they would cut into strips, salt, and hang out to dry.

Crouching, Davy probed the murky undergrowth for a telltale hint of movement. Unsuccessful, he inched to the left, tucking the stock of his long rifle to his shoulder. No other sounds broke the stillness. Even the breeze had momentarily dwindled.

A whisper of motion to the west brought Davy around in a twinkling. Somehow, the animal had snuck past him. Or were there two of them? Hunkering, he bided his time, knowing that most animals gave themselves away sooner or later.

Not in this instance, however. Davy let a full five minutes go by, then rose and glided deeper into the brush. Apparently the animal had eluded him, because he found no trace of it.

Just then a rustling noise sounded to the south. Jarred by the realization that he had made a grievous blunder, Davy spun.

It was no deer. Whatever lurked in the gathering gloom was circling him, stalking him. The hunter had become the hunted. But what was it? Davy mentally ticked off the possibilities: a bear, a painter, one of the wolves, maybe even a wolverine.

His best bet was to reach the meadow. In the open he could see it charge.

Backpedaling, never taking his gaze off the thicket where the sound came from, Davy threaded through the trees. It was so dark when he reached the meadow that he could barely see his hand at arm's length.

No snarling brute burst from cover. Nothing tried to stop him.

"Where's our meal?" Flavius asked, profoundly disappointed that his friend was returning empty-handed. The only aspect of their journey that made it bearable, in his opinion, were the delicious hot suppers Davy whipped up. Having to resort to jerky and pemmican *again* was plumb depressing.

Practically everyone in western Tennessee knew about Flavius's fondness for food. His pie-eating ability was legendary. One year, he'd won every contest in four counties. It got so that no one would compete with him; the outcome was a foregone conclusion.

"Sorry. I couldn't find anything," Davy said. He debated whether to tell Flavius what had happened, and decided not to. Flavius would only fret himself sick. And it was unlikely that any roving beast would dare come near their fire.

Sitting, Davy poured himself a cup of coffee from the pot Flavius had brewed. They were out of sugar so he drank it black, savoring the warmth that spread through his midsection.

"Wonderful," Flavius muttered, sulking. To date he had lost close to ten pounds. At the rate they were going, he'd be skin and bones when they finally reached Tennessee.

To cheer his friend, Davy made small talk. They reminisced about their wives and Davy's children, about their homesteads and kin. They discussed politics, which had always held a strange fascination for Davy but bored Flavius to death.

"Politicians!" he spat at one point. "They're all a bunch of swindlers. And those that ain't are power hungry." He shook his head. "Mark my words. This country would be better off if we only let Congress sit in session two days out of the year."

"How do you figure?" Davy asked, taking a bite of tangy jerky.

"That's all the time it would take Congress to pass new laws we actually need. The rest of the time those strutting peacocks just flap their gums to hear themselves talk."

Davy didn't argue the point. It wasn't the institution that should be blamed, it was the people who belonged to it. A decent man, someone who represented the interests of the common folk and not the special interests or the greedy, could do some real good.

The fire was burning low. Davy placed his tin cup down and turned to add more wood.

"I'll be back in a while," Flavius said, standing and hitching at his belt.

"Don't forget your rifle."

"Never," Flavius said.

A frontiersman's rifle was as essential to his survival as his legs and arms. More essential, in fact, since a man could get by without a limb but he could hardly fend off a ravenous grizzly or a bloodthirsty war party without a gun.

It explained why trans-Appalachian frontiersmen were so fond of their Kentucky rifles, so fond that they gave their guns pet names.

Blood Hunt

Davy watched the darkness swallow Flavius. Hours had gone by since his encounter in the woods, so he was not concerned for his companion's welfare.

Sparks wafted skyward as Davy added a thick branch to the flames. Overhead sparkled a myriad of stars, a breathtaking spectacle that always mightily stirred Davy's soul. He lay back, his arms folded behind his head. The tail on his coonskin cap brushed his wrist.

Lord, the heavens were beautiful! Davy noted the Big Dipper and the North Star. He saw Mars. Plus several constellations.

It never ceased to astound him how creation was so orderly, how the stars and the planets were part of a vast stellar procession that performed as smoothly as a steam engine.

The sight was proof, if any were needed, that the Almighty existed. Davy knew there were some people who claimed that existence was an accident, that random chance had given birth to everything. But how could you get something out of nothing? No, they were wrong, and one day—

The sorrel raised its head and nickered. Instantly Davy was on his knees, Liz in hand. Both horses were peering in the direction Harris had gone.

"Flavius?" Davy called quietly. On not receiving a response, he stood and skirted the crackling fire. It had been a mistake to sit facing the flames. Now his eyes needed time to adjust.

"Flavius?" Davy called once again, but louder. Surely his friend would not go far. He took another step.

The patter of onrushing feet brought Davy around in a blur. But as fast as he was, he was not quite quick enough. He caught a glimpse of a tall Indian

17

wearing some sort of turban headdress and tried to bring Liz to bear, but the warrior was on him in a long bound. A bony shoulder rammed into his chest, bowling him over.

Somehow Davy held on to his rifle. Rolling when he landed, he shoved up into a crouch and leveled Liz. A flashing war club slammed against the barrel, swatting the gun from his grasp. He ducked under a blow that would have flattened him like a board, and clawed for a pistol.

Suddenly, iron arms encircled Davy from behind. He was yanked to his feet, and the man holding him barked instructions in an unfamiliar tongue.

The warrior armed with the war club raised it to strike. Tensing, Davy coiled his legs. As the club arced forward, he wrenched sharply to one side, swinging the man behind him around. A thud and a cry of anguish rewarded his ploy.

The arms gripping him slackened. Exerting all his strength, Davy burst free. Whirling, he unlimbered his tomahawk. The first man was already renewing his assault, while the second was bent over, clutching his ribs.

War club and Creek tomahawk clashed. The tomahawk was considerably smaller, but backed by Davy's powerful sinews, it deflected the club. Davy followed through with a backhand swipe that clipped the tall Indian on the temple. Unfortunately, only the flat of the tomahawk connected, or he would have opened the man's head like a ripe melon.

A yip from the bent-over warrior brought two more barreling out of the night. One held a lance; the other's hands were empty.

Davy pivoted to meet their attack. In doing so he had to take his eyes off the man with the club. He parried a thrust of the lance and drove his fist full into the warrior's jaw. The Indian crumpled. Before Davy could capitalize, he was tackled across the shins.

His shoulder blades hit the ground hard. Davy kicked but the warrior clung on. He hoisted the tomahawk, only to have it batted from his grasp by the other Indian's war club. Jerking to the left, he felt the club brush his shoulder.

Four against one were impossible odds. Unless Davy broke free, he would suffer Flavius's fate. For he had no doubt that his friend had gone to meet their Maker. And it was all his fault. He had talked Flavius into coming. If not for him, the portly Tennessean would be safe and snug in his cabin right about then.

The man who was holding Davy's legs grabbed for Davy's knife. Blocking the lunge, Davy pummeled the warrior's head and shoulders. All the while he evaded the war club, which hissed perilously near his ears.

In desperation, Davy gouged his fingers into the warrior's eyes. Howling, the man let go, enabling Davy to surge up off the grass and resort to a flintlock. Without warning, a keg of black powder exploded in his skull. The world spun. The fire danced crazily.

The thump Davy felt was his body crashing to earth. Vaguely, he sensed that someone had seized his buckskin shirt and flipped him over. Dimly, he saw a knife lowering toward his exposed throat.

Davy's last thoughts were of his wife and sprouts. Elizabeth was a strong woman. She would make do. But she would go to her grave questioning why he

David Thompson

had always been traipsing off to parts unknown. "Someday," she had once mentioned, "your galli-vants will be the death of you."

Damned if she hadn't been right!

Chapter Two

The sensation of being violently shaken was the first inkling Davy Crockett had that he was still alive. Dizzily, he swam up from the unplumbed depths of an inky, icy well.

Fingers were entwined in his shirt. Someone breathed heavily above him.

Thinking that it was one of the warriors about to finish him off, Davy shot out his right arm as his eyes snapped open. His hand closed around the fleshy throat of the man looming above him.

"Davy! It's me!" Flavius Harris squawked, fearing that his neck would be crushed before his friend realized what he was doing.

"Flavius?" Davy said thickly. Relaxing his grip, he struggled to clear clinging cobwebs from his brain. His friend helped him to sit up.

"Land o' Goshen! I thought you were a goner for sure!" Flavius declared. "I saw that heathen go to slit

21

your throat, but there was nothing I could do."

"What stopped him, then?" Davy asked, scanning their campsite for sign of the Indians. They were gone. So were the horses and blankets. His saddle was there, but Harris's had disappeared.

"That tall feller with the club saved your bacon. He grabbed the arm of the one who was about to cut you. They spatted some, then the one with the knife got up and stomped off, as mad as a wet hen."

Davy tried to stand, but it was too soon. His head spun. A nasty knot, bleeding slightly, would remind him of the clash for days to come. If not for his thick coonskin cap, he would have been much worse off.

Flavius was so relieved that his friend was alive, his eyes moistened. Coughing, he said, "They jumped me in the woods. I never stood a prayer. The one with the club bashed me on the noggin, and the next thing I knew, I was lying there all by my lonesome, with my rifle and my knife and my possibles gone."

Davy looked down. His own weapons and powder horn and ammo pouch had been taken.

"I came as quick as I could. Saw them scoop up our blankets, tote my saddle off, and lead our horses that-a-way." Flavius bobbed his head northward.

"How long ago?"

Flavius shrugged. "Five minutes, maybe. I had a heck of a time bringing you around."

"Why did they steal the saddle?" Davy puzzled aloud. As a general rule, Indians disliked the white man's version. Most tribes either had no use for saddles whatsoever, or relied on small leather versions stuffed with buffalo hair or grass.

Other aspects of the attack were equally strange. A war club was capable of crushing a man's skull. Most frontiersmen would rather be shot than hit by one, because nine times out of ten a war club proved fatal.

Yet the tall warrior had struck Flavius and him, both, and they were still alive. Either the man was incredibly puny, or he had deliberately not slain them. Which was a ridiculous notion. Why would a member of a war party spare his mortal enemies?

Davy saw his cap and put it on, careful of the knot. Maybe the notion wasn't as silly as he thought. Flavius had seen the tall warrior stop the other one from slitting his jugular. Again, why? It made no sense.

"What do we do now?" Flavius asked. Stranded on foot, without provisions and weapons, they would be lucky to get out of the wilderness alive.

"What else?" Davy said, attempting a second time to rise. Both temples throbbed, but this time he succeeded. "At first light we go after them."

Flavius blinked. "That conk must have cracked your brainpan. How in hell can we catch them when they have our horses?"

"Think it through. Two horses, four men. They'll have to ride double, or else take turns," Davy explained. "Either way, it'll slow them down. If we hustle, we can catch them."

"Great!" Flavius said, although he was less than excited at the prospect of going up against the quartet unarmed.

Davy was not fooled. His friend had a habit of shying from danger. Not that Davy blamed him. After the horrible atrocities he had witnessed during the Creek War, atrocities committed by both sides, he'd had his fill of bloodletting.

It wouldn't bother Davy one bit to live the rest of his days and not take another human life, red or white. He was being unrealistic, though. Bloodshed was all too common on the frontier. The white man and the red just couldn't get along no matter how hard they tried.

Davy's grandfather and grandmother had been early casualties. The Creeks had wiped them out. He'd also lost cousins, friends, acquaintances.

That was enough to make almost anyone an inveterate Indian-hater. And for a while Davy had despised them as much as any white. Then he had gone on a hunt with some friends, and fallen sick. His so-called friends had left him to die.

Some Indians had found him. Indians who did not know him from Adam. Indians who could have easily killed him and never been caught. Yet they had looked after him, had taken him a long distance to the nearest settler.

Davy owed his life to those red men. He had no idea who they were. He'd never been able to thank them. But now, whenever he heard fellow whites insist that the red race be exterminated, he remembered those Indians.

The fire had burned low. Davy built it up and slid his saddle closer. Without blankets, they would be quite cold by morning. "We should get some rest," he commented.

Flavius tried, but he was too nervous to sleep. He felt too vulnerable, too helpless. Just like when he had been a small boy, and had lain in his bed late at night trembling in fear, terrified that ogres and trolls and demons would leap out of the darkness to devour him.

Curling up as close to the flames as he dared, Flavius listened for the stealthy pad of approaching beasts. Or maybe the war party would return to finish what they had started.

It didn't help matters that the night came alive with noise. Wolves howled. Bears grunted. Cougars snarled and shrieked. Flavius tried to ignore them. His heavy eyelids drooped, and he was on the verge of falling asleep when something huge crashed through the undergrowth east of the meadow. Leaping to his feet, he braced for the worst. But whatever it was ran off in the opposite direction, spooked by their fire.

Davy slept soundly the whole time. How he did it, Flavius would never know. Lying down, he grasped an unused piece of firewood. It wasn't much, but he could defend himself with it. Gradually, he drifted off, only to be startled awake minutes later by a hand on his shoulder.

Minutes, did he think? Streaks of pink and yellow painted the eastern sky. Birds chirped gaily in the trees, greeting the new day with their morning ritual.

"Time to go," Davy said. They must not waste any time. Indians were early risers. The war party would be under way by sunrise.

"What about your saddle?" Flavius inquired.

Davy was loath to leave it behind. Animals might damage it, or someone might steal it, and saddles were not cheap. Concealing it in the undergrowth was his only option. He stooped to grab the saddle horn—and stiffened.

The forest had become completely quiet. Every bird had hushed: every robin, every sparrow, every jay, every finch.

Flavius noticed, and pushed erect. Only two things could silence the avian chorus so abruptly: a roving predator or other humans in the vicinity. Which was it?

An answer came in the form of a harsh shout from the woodland. "Don't move! Either of you! So much as lift a finger, and we'll riddle you!"

Without thinking, elated at their good fortune,

Flavius took a step, crying out, "They're white men, Davy! We're safe now!"

The crack of a shot proved otherwise. A puff of smoke blossomed, marking the shooter's position, even as the earth in front of Flavius's right toe erupted in a miniature geyser.

"We won't warn you again!" bellowed the man in the woods. "The next ball goes right between your eyes."

Davy had not budged. "Do as they say," he cautioned. "If they're cutthroats, we don't have anything worth stealing. They might leave us alone."

Cutthroats? Flavius paled. Several bands of brigands had been plaguing the frontier for years, preying on isolated farm families and unwary travelers. Could Fate be so cruel as to put their lives at risk again so soon after the Indian attack?

Figures materialized out of the shadows under the trees on both sides of the meadow. Davy counted: . . . seven, eight, nine. Most wore homespun clothes, a few buckskins. All held rifles and wore expressions that hinted they were eager to squeeze the trigger.

A man with the build of an ox was in the fore. The barrel of his Kentucky did not waver as he crossed to within five yards of the Tennesseans and scrutinized them intently. "The jig is up, bastards. I bet you didn't think we'd be so close behind them, did you?"

The men formed a ring. An older frontiersman, his hair spiked with gray, lowered his rifle's muzzle and said, "Hold on, Cyrus. These two aren't 'breeds."

"So?" Cyrus retorted. "They helped those filthy Injuns, didn't they? If we had the time, I'd stake them out, peel their hides, and wait for the buzzards to show. But as it is, we ought to shoot them where they stand."

Flavius had no idea what was going on. But the

remark about the Indians spurred him into moving toward the stocky woodsman and saying, "Hold on a second, friend. You have us pegged all wrong. We—"

A growl tore from Cyrus's throat. The stock of his rifle whipped around, driving into Flavius's stomach with so much force, Flavius swore his spine was broken. Wheezing and sputtering, Flavius tottered, then sank to his knees. Cyrus raised the stock high.

"No!" the older man cried, leaping between them. "Damn it, Cy! I understand your grief. But we can't punish these men without proof. We have to let them have their say."

A third frontiersman, a weasel of a man whose thin mustache had been oiled and tweaked until it resembled a cat's whiskers, motioned for the old man to move aside. "Out of the way, Norval. We ain't got time to waste."

Davy had been studying the newcomers. Their clothes were in reasonably fine shape, clean and mended in spots. That indicated a woman's touch. Several sported neatly trimmed beards. The rest had stubble on their chins, but no more than two days' worth, if that. These were ordinary settlers, not a band of scruffy cutthroats.

"If you're after the Indians who jumped us last night," Davy said, "we'd be obliged if you would return our horses and effects when you catch them."

The man called Norval turned. "That's a Southern accent, or I'm the Queen of England. Where are you boys from?"

"Tennessee," Davy revealed.

A lanky frontiersmen with a pointed chin, who was reloading his rifle, glanced up. "You're a long way from home, feller. What brings you to our neck of the woods?"

Davy fibbed. "We're looking to move our families up in this area. We came to explore the countryside." They might not believe him if he admitted that a hankering to see new sights was to blame. No one in their right mind would travel clear from Tennessee to northern Illinois, and beyond, on a whim. No one but him, that was.

Cyrus snorted. "He's lyin', Kayne. As any fool can see."

The lanky man's gray eyes glittered. "I see no such thing. Does that make *me* a fool?"

An air of latent menace radiated from the woodsman known as Kayne, as obvious as the thinly veiled threat in his tone. Davy noted that Cyrus promptly pulled in his horns.

"No. Not at all. Don't go puttin' words in my mouth, damn it."

Flavius slowly stood. The agony in his gut had almost subsided, and he could breathe again. He sorely wished he could give Cyrus a punch in the mouth for the outrage. "What's wrong with you people?" he demanded. "Is this how folks in these parts greet strangers?" He sniffed. "First those redskins, now this! I can't wait to be shed of here."

Cyrus glowered spitefully. "What's your name, fat man?"

It was a mistake. If there was one insult Flavius would not abide, it was that. He'd stand for being called plump, or portly, or even uncommonly stout. But never *fat*. For the truth was that his ample girth packed more muscle than anything else. Pivoting, Flavius jabbed a finger at Cyrus and snapped, "Put down that rifle, mister, and I'll show you how we teach jackasses like you proper manners back in Tennessee."

"Why, you—!" Cyrus hefted his rifle and lunged, but Norval pushed against his chest.

"Enough! We're on urgent business, remember?"

Cyrus sobered, but he did not look happy. "I'll let it pass, for now. When this is over, though, fatty will answer to me."

Davy picked that moment to smile and offer his hand to Kayne. When the lanky frontiersman stepped forward to shake, Davy introduced himself, adding, "I'd be grateful if you would tell me what this is all about."

Kayne pushed his flat-brimmed black hat back on his head. "We're from Peoria, mister. It's a new settlement not far to the south. The day before last, Indians raided a cabin on the outskirts. They made off with a woman."

"Dear Lord." Being taken captive by Indians was what every female on the frontier dreaded more than anything else. Only a few were ever rescued. Some were eventually ransomed, but out of shame and grief found it hard to adapt to being back among their own kind. The majority were never heard of again. "How old is she? Is she in good health?"

"What difference does that make?" Cyrus testily cut in.

"All the difference in the world," Davy calmly replied. "If she's elderly or can't hold her own for some reason, and you get too close, they're liable to make wolf meat of her. They won't let her slow them down."

"Rebecca is twenty-two," Norval said. "She's my niece. They jumped my brother when he was out working in the fields, and knocked him out. His wife tried to fight them off, but they pushed her down and dragged off the screaming girl."

"They didn't kill anyone?" Davy asked.

Norval shook his head. "That's the odd part. They

went out of their way not to harm a soul."

Flavius realized why Davy had asked the question. "Hey! They did the same thing with us. Those devils could have butchered us both, but they didn't touch a hair on our heads."

"Awful peculiar," Davy commented. As a rule, war parties massacred every white they came across. Why were these Indians so different? he wondered.

Kayne had finished reloading and replaced his ramrod. Facing Cyrus and the weasel, he said, "Do you still reckon these two are in cahoots with the Injuns?"

Flavius was insulted by the suggestion. "Are you addlepated? What white man would be in league with a bunch of red fiends?"

"There are a few," Kayne said.

Norval elaborated. "Peoria was started by 'breeds and whites who set up an outpost to trade with the Indians. Even after most of the Indians turned hostile, they stayed on friendly terms. Too friendly, if you take my meaning."

Kayne nodded. "Decent homesteaders moved in, and when there were enough of us, we drove the riffraff out. They didn't take kindly to it, but there wasn't much they could do."

"Except make our lives miserable every chance they get," Cyrus said bitterly.

"So you can see why we were suspicious of you," Norval told Davy. "It wasn't personal. We figured that you had been waiting here with horses so the kidnappers could get away."

"What tribe are these Indians?" Davy asked.

"Sauks," Norval said. "Or Sacs, as some like to call them."

Cyrus, fidgeting impatiently, swore. "What damn difference does it make whether they're Sauk, Fox,

Chippewa, Kickapoo, Mascouten, or Shawnee? Injuns are Injuns. We should wipe out every warrior, squaw, and nit."

There it was again. The warped outlook that Davy could never agree with, not in a million years. "We'd be grateful if you'd let us tag along," he offered tactfully.

"What good would you be?" rasped the weasel. "You don't even have a gun."

"I can track some," Davy allowed.

"John Kayne is our tracker," Norval said. "He's the best in these parts. If he doesn't mind your help, your welcome to join us."

The lanky frontiersman smiled. "It don't make me no never mind. Just so you can move quiet-like."

"Then it's settled," Cyrus said. "Let's get going. Every second we waste, we fall farther behind."

Davy swung his saddle over his shoulder and followed the Illinoisans as they hastened northward. Norval pointed out each of the men by name. Only the weasel, whose name was Dilbert, and Cyrus betrayed resentment at having Flavius and him join the rescue party.

Hiding the saddle took only a few moments. Davy slid it into a briar patch and covered it with weeds he ripped out by the roots. Satisfied no one would find it, he jogged to catch up with the others, who had not waited. Dilbert shot him a dirty look as he ran past and joined John Kayne.

The tracker was stooped low, examining tufts of bent grass and horse tacks. "Here's where they mounted up. They put your saddle on the biggest horse and had Rebecca climb on."

"That would be my bay," Davy said. The sorrel was two hands smaller, its tracks correspondingly smaller.

"One of the warriors climbed on the other animal, and off they went," Kayne said. A grunt escaped him. "Look here. The other two are running behind. So they won't be going much faster than we can."

Davy spied two sets of prints that puzzled him. "What do you make of these?" he asked. One set had been made by the captive. The other set had been made by a Sauk. They had stood facing each other, almost toe to toe. What attracted his interest was that the impressions of the woman's toes were sunk in deeper than they normally would be, as if she had leaned on the warrior for support. Was she hurt?

John Kayne took one look and his features clouded. He shifted position so that none of the others could see his face, then whispered, "You're the genuine article, Crockett. Ain't many would have caught on. Do me a favor and don't tell anyone, hear?"

Davy did not understand the need for secrecy, but he nodded and fell into step beside Kayne. They moved rapidly, making no more noise than would a prowling panther. Sticking to the war party's trail was no great feat; the hoofprints made it easy.

The morning waxed and waned. Davy's rumbling stomach reminded him that he had not eaten breakfast, but he did not ask to stop. Saving the woman was more important. He had been on rescue missions before and knew that the first two or three days after an abduction took place were crucial. If the rescuers failed to catch up by then, it was virtually certain they never would.

Noon came and went. About an hour later the settlers crested a rise. A tree-covered slope brought them to a clearing beside a gurgling creek.

"We're in luck!" Kayne said. "They stopped here to rest a spell and water the horses. We can't be more than four or five miles behind them now."

"Then what are we waitin' for?" grated Cyrus. Striding to the water's edge, he beckoned. "Come on, boys! Push on hard, and we'll have her back by nightfall!"

Norval made a clucking sound. "Not so fast, Cy. We've been on the go since yesterday morning, and we're tuckered out. Those Injuns had the right idea. I say we rest half an hour. From then on, we won't stop until Rebecca is safe and sound or we drop dead from exhaustion."

"That's too long," Cyrus said. "Fifteen minutes is all we can spare."

At Davy's quizzical glance, Kayne spoke in a hushed tone so no one else would overhear. "Rebecca's pa pledged her hand to Cy a month ago."

"They're lovers?" Davy said. It shed a new light on Cy's attitude. Any man whose beloved was in the clutches of hostiles was bound to be as prickly as a porcupine.

"I wouldn't say that, exactly," Kayne said.

Cyrus and Norval had not stopped spatting. Davy resolved their dispute by rising and saying, "My partner and I aren't that tired. We'll go on ahead. If we spot the Sauks before you overtake us, one of us will fly back and let you know while the other keeps them in sight."

Flavius was on his knees at the creek, cooling his neck and face. "We will?" he said, annoyed that Davy had volunteered his services without consulting him. The brawny Irishman tended to forget that few people possessed his steely stamina. Flavius was about to remind him, when around a bend to the northwest floated an object that jolted him so badly he forgot all about complaining.

It was a headless body.

Chapter Three

Flavius Harris had witnessed more than his share of grisly sights. During the Creek War he had been with a scouting party that found a butchered settler. The man had been skinned alive, his eyes gouged out, his tongue cut off. Another time he had looked on while a Creek warrior was interrogated by soldiers under Andrew Jackson's command, and the things those fellows did to that Indian made him half sick whenever he recalled it.

So the body in the stream was not the most gruesome horror Flavius ever beheld. But coming so unexpectedly as it did, Flavius was momentarily jarred speechless. Long enough for the headless corpse to float almost within arm's reach. Long enough for the jagged stump of a neck with its pinkish flesh and the gleaming white of severed vertebrae to indelibly impress itself in his memory.

Most of the others had their backs to the stream.

Blood Hunt

Davy Crockett turned to ford it and saw his friend gaping in sickly dismay. A glance, and he bounded into the water to grab the body by the wrist before it floated on past the clearing. "Here! What's this!" he called out to the rest.

Norval, Cyrus, Dilbert, and company dashed over. John Kayne lent a hand hauling the heavy bulk out. Kayne then knelt to inspect the elaborately worked buckskins, the hands, and especially the moccasins of the deceased. "It was a Sauk," he pronounced.

"Are you sure?" one of the men asked.

Kayne tapped the buckskin leggings. "No two tribes make their clothes alike, Hillman. This is a Sauk warrior, all right."

Davy touched a bronzed hand that lay palm up. Judging by how warm and limber the fingers were, the body had not been in the water very long. "Maybe it's one of those we've been following," he speculated.

"But who could have done it?" Cyrus said. "There are no other whites in this area that I know of."

Kayne grimly stood. "Who said anything about it being whites? The tribes hereabouts are always at each other's throats."

"That's right," Norval said. "The Sauk and the Fox are bitter enemies of the Chippewa and the Dakota."

"And there are all those other hostiles up in Canada," Dilbert added. "These red vermin breed like rabbits, I tell you."

Cyrus stared at the body and gulped. "But if the band that stole my Rebecca was jumped by another war party, what happened to Rebecca?"

Davy and Kayne swapped looks. The same question had already occurred to both of them. After quickly fording the stream, they searched the ground. It took but a few seconds to prove what Davy feared. "They never came out on this side," he reported.

"What does that mean?" Hillman asked. He was a big-boned, husky frontiersman whose wits were slower than trickling tree sap.

Kayne pointed at the bend around which the body had appeared. "It means they went up the middle of the stream to throw us off the scent."

Cyrus stepped into the water. "What are we waitin' for? Rebecca might be lyin' out there somewhere with *her* head hacked off."

No one disputed him. Davy and Kayne assumed the lead, each probing a bank.

Now that they were close to the Indians, Flavius made a point of staying near his friend. In a battle, Davy was a rip-snortin' terror who sliced through his enemies like a scythe through grain. Flavius had seen Davy so caught up in the swirl of combat that he forgot to watch his back. So Flavius took that job on himself.

The woods were quiet. Unnaturally so. Davy ran his keen eyes over every blade of grass, every weed. Patches of bare dirt bore plenty of prints. Raccoons, deer, bobcats, bear, possums, and many other animals had all slaked their thirst at one time or another.

The water was cold, but not unbearably so. Davy's high moccasins, superbly crafted by his wife, were thicker than most, and had spared him from frostbite and worse on many an occasion.

Davy took great pride in his wife's craftsmanship. On the frontier, women had the burden of providing almost all the clothing their families wore. A wife's ability determined whether her family was warm in the winter and comfortable in the summer.

Like most Tennessee backwoodsmen, Davy usually wore a long deerskin hunting shirt, open at the neck. It was banded at the waist by his wide leather belt. Buckskin trousers fell almost to the soles of his feet and were split at the front hem to fit snugly over his moccasins.

A furrow on the bank brought Davy to a stop. A check disclosed that it had been made by a fawn scrambling out of the stream, not by a human foot.

Davy went on. The water swished around his legs with every step. A frog leaped from a log, diving deep. Shortly thereafter a garter snake slithered into the undergrowth.

The rescuers traveled over a mile from the clearing. They rounded a bend choked by thickets. A wide pool broadened before them, shaded by overhanging boughs.

Bearing to the right, Davy spotted trampled grass a few yards from the stream and climbed out to investigate. A small scarlet puddle fringed a moccasin print. Beyond were more tracks, many more, clear evidence of a terrific struggle. "Take a gander at this," he said.

Flavius was glad to leave the water. His toes felt half frozen. Even worse, he was hungry enough to eat a whole cow with all the trimmings. His stomach rumbled constantly, embarrassing him no end. He hoped that now they would take the time to eat, but no one brought up the subject of food.

Davy moved in ever-wider circles, reading the tracks. The sequence of events was as plain as the nose on his face.

The Sauks and their captive had stopped to rest. Both horses had been allowed to graze and had wandered some thirty feet away. Unknown to the Sauks, skulkers in the trees had watched everything closely.

Evidently, another war party had heard them coming and hidden. The second band was much larger. Eleven warriors, by Davy's reckoning. They had probably waited until the Sauks were completely off guard, then burst from concealment. One of the Sauks had gone down in the initial rush. Another had been wounded.

Fighting furiously, the Sauks had retreated into the stream. Why the larger band had not gone after them, Davy could not fathom. But the evidence proved that they hadn't. He went across, confirming that three of the Sauks had made it to safety, the wounded man being assisted by another.

The captive and the horses had been left in the clutches of the second war party. A large circle of red grass marked where they had chopped the head from the Sauk who had fallen. Finger impressions in the soil indicated that the man had still been alive.

Afterward, the larger war party had lost no time in departing. Their trail led to the northwest.

John Kayne had been doing the same as Davy. Now he hunkered beside a pair of footprints and scratched his chin. "These are new ones on me," he remarked.

"What is?" Hillman asked.

"No two tribes make their moccasins exactly alike," Kayne explained. "I thought I knew all the kinds ever seen in our territory, but I've never come across any like these before. My guess would be it's a band from up in Canada, snuck down to count coup, as the Dakotas like to say."

"God, no!" Cyrus said. "They'll take Rebecca north of the border! I'll never see her again!"

Norval placed a hand on the younger settler's shoulder. "Calm down. It's a long way to the border. We'll catch them."

Davy was not as optimistic. The band from Canada

would be anxious to reach their own country before the Sauks retaliated. It could explain why they had not gone after the three Sauks who escaped. The attackers wrongly supposed that the trio were part of a bigger war party which might arrive at any minute.

Rebecca was added incentive to speedy flight. To be caught with a white woman would bring down on the band the full fury of every white settler within two hundred miles.

"We'll have to push harder than ever," Davy declared.

John Kayne hitched at his belt. "The two of us will go on ahead. We'll blaze a trail as we go."

Flavius did not care to be separated from his friend. "I'm going too," he stated. His belly picked that instant to imitate a ravenous bruin, and everyone heard. Dilbert and a couple others smirked.

"If you want," Kayne said. "But you'll have to keep up."

The implication peeved Flavius. "Don't fret in that regard. I can hold my own."

Davy came to his friend's defense. "Don't let his looks fool you, Kayne. My partner has more real grit than most ten men. During the Creek War he once went two whole days without a bite to eat or anything to drink. He marched through gator-infested swamps and snake-infested bogs without a lick of complaint. I'd stack him up against any man, any day of the week."

"I'll take your word for it," Kayne said.

Under different circumstances, Flavius would have made an issue of the insult. His entire life, he'd had to put up with people poking fun at him or insulting him because of the girth of his waist. It was unfair.

Just because someone was heftier than normal didn't mean that person was a slug.

Kayne plunged into the forest. Davy clapped Flavius on the back, whispered, "Don't let them get your goat!" and whisked into the undergrowth.

Flavius was hard-pressed to keep up with them. Gritting his teeth, he knuckled down, ignoring the pangs in his calves and the sweat that rolled off him in waves. He consoled himself with the notion that his suffering was for a noble cause.

The Canadian Indians had held to a northeasterly course for quite some time, then bore northward. They had made Rebecca ride the sorrel, but no one rode the bay.

Davy adopted a jogging rhythm that ate up the miles. Although tired, he never suggested they stop. Although hungry, he never gave consideration to food.

Wondering about the captive preoccupied him. What must that poor woman be going through? Davy mused. For her, being abducted by the new band must be like going from the frying pan into the fire. The Sauks, at least, were native to that region. Who knew where the new war party would take her?

The depth of her despair was a crucial factor. If she had spunk and spirit, she could hold her own until help arrived. But if she was prone to melancholy, if she believed her plight was hopeless, she might take her own life.

Others had done so. Whites dreaded being at the mercy of hostile Indians. Lurid tales of torture and slaughter abounded, made vastly more disturbing by the realization they were for the most part true. It was why so many pioneers, women and men, killed themselves rather than be taken captive.

The worst case Davy ever heard of involved the wife of a farmer and her six children. When Creeks pounced on her man while he was out plowing, she barricaded herself and her brood in their cabin. The Creeks wanted them alive and made no attempt to burn them out.

On the third day of the siege, heartbroken and overwhelmed by abject despair, the woman had fed her offspring johnnycakes laced with poison, then put the muzzle of a flintlock pistol into her mouth and blown the top of her head off.

Later, when the Indians broke in, they did not mutilate her out of respect for her courage.

The memory sparked Davy into quietly asking, "Kayne, what sort of woman is this Rebecca?"

"She's as fine as they come," the lanky backwoodsman replied without breaking stride. "Strong-willed, yet tenderhearted. Spirited, but not headstrong. Calm in a crisis. Easygoing with kids. The best cook and quilt maker this side of the Mississippi. And the prettiest gal you'd ever want to meet." He paused. "Not the type to kill herself, if that's what you're thinking."

"I was," Davy admitted. He was also thinking that seldom had he heard such a glowing description of anyone. "You sound right fond of her," he diplomatically phrased it.

"All the single men in Peoria would give their eyeteeth to be in Cyrus's boots," Kayne said. "Rebecca Worthington is as fine a woman as ever drew breath."

"She must have had a heap of suitors," Davy said. "How did Cyrus win out?"

For a while Kayne did not answer. When he did, he spat the words as if they were tacks. "Festus, her father, has the final say. And Cyrus's pa owns the trading post."

A few feet to the rear, Flavius could not help eaves-

41

dropping. The connection eluded him. "So? What does that have to do with anything?"

"So Cyrus's pa is the richest man around. Once he passes on, Cyrus, an only child, inherits the whole boodle. Festus likes the idea of having a rich son-in-law."

Flavius was appalled. "He's forcing his daughter to marry that ox? How does Rebecca feel about the arrangement?"

"She's not the type to air private grievances. But she did confide to my youngest sister that she can't stand to be in the same room as Cy. The rumor is that she cares for someone else, that she's been secretly in love with this other man for a long time."

"Who's the lucky man?" Flavius inquired.

"No one knows. My sister thinks it must be someone who's been at the settlement quite a spell, because Rebecca let it slip that the man she adores was one of the first to greet her family when they arrived."

Davy's hearing was second to none. He never missed the distant crack of twigs or the slightest inflections in a tone. "How long have you been at Peoria?" he quizzed.

"Longer than most," Kayne said, and let it go at that.

The rescue was taking on whole new dimensions. Troubling dimensions, because men who were ruled by their hearts instead of their heads frequently made fatal mistakes.

How many other members of the rescue party, Davy wondered, felt as Kayne did? It had not dawned on him before, but all the rescuers were young except for Norval, Festus's brother. Were they all smitten?

Kayne slowed to better read the tracks as they crossed a stretch of rocky soil.

"Why didn't her father join you?" Davy asked.

"He wanted to, but he had a gash in his head the size of your thumb. Kept seeing double. In a few days he should be fit enough to travel, and he promised to follow us with a dozen more men."

By then their trail would be cold. Even if they were guided by a man of Kayne's caliber and savvy, it would be many days before Festus's bunch joined them. By then Rebecca's fate would be sealed.

The afternoon crawled by, weighted by millstones. Every now and again Kayne or Davy cut bark from a tree to guide Norval and the boys.

Flavius fell a little behind. It had been a coon's age since he last covered so much distance so briskly, afoot, and his muscles protested. His legs stiffened up on him.

The chattering of an irate squirrel made Flavius wish he could squeeze off a shot. Just one. He could see the animal prancing on a high limb, taunting him. He envisioned it skinned and cleaned and chopped into bits, simmering enticingly in a pot.

The war party from Canada had stuck to a winding game trail for a while. Flavius followed along, giving scant regard to his companions until he raised his head and there they were right in front of him. Both had stopped and were gazing at something ahead.

Curious, Flavius shouldered between them. Someone gasped, and he realized it was him. For jammed onto the top of a long length of trimmed branch and left smack in the game trail for them to discover was the severed head of the Sauk warrior whose body had been thrown into the stream.

The lips had discolored, the tongue was protruding. Glazed eyes were fixed blankly on them. Flies buzzed thickly around the gory trophy.

The warrior had been young, no older than

twenty-five. High cheekbones framed a large, hawk-ish nose. An odd turbanlike affair had been wound across his brow and around his head.

"What in the world is this for?" Flavius said, his stomach churning.

"It's a warning," Davy guessed. "They know some-one is after them and they're telling us to give up, or else."

"Why'd they pick this spot?" Kayne said.

"No special reason, I imagine," Flavius responded.

Davy had his doubts. Indians rarely did anything on a whim. He surveyed the woodland and smiled to himself. At that point the forest thinned. A gap in the trees enabled him to spy a hill a quarter of a mile away. Anyone on it would be able to see them. Not clearly, mind, but well enough to know how many they were, and whether they were white or red. "They're onto us," he said.

Kayne tore his eyes from the head, saw the hill, and flushed in anger. "Damn! I should have swung wide. We'll never take them by surprise now."

"Don't give up hope," Davy said. "They'll expect us to continue along the game trail. What if we don't?"

Comprehension lit Kayne's countenance. "It'll be risky. There's no telling how many are lying in wait for us."

Once again Flavius was unsure of what they had in mind. But he was positive that he wouldn't like it. Davy had a knack for getting them into hot water. "What's the plan?"

"We'll keep going a ways," Davy said. "Two of us will break off when the woods hem us in and circle around behind the hill. The third man will jog on up the trail, sort of as bait. With any luck, the war party won't realize what we've done until it's too late."

Flavius's mouth became as dry as a desert. "Which

44

one of us will be the decoy?" As if he couldn't guess.

"If you don't want to, just say so," Davy said. "We're just a mite more spry than you, is all." It pained him to be so brutally blunt, but lives were riding on their ruse.

"I need this like I need a pig in my hip pocket," Flavius muttered. Setting himself up as a living target was nit-brained. Yet if it saved the woman, he'd make the sacrifice. "I reckon I've got it to do," he reluctantly acknowledged.

Davy squeezed his friend's arm and said, "Go slow and make enough noise to convince them the three of us are together. Stop if you have to, but only when you can't see the hill."

"Just don't dally," Flavius said. They moved on, leaving the head where it was. Flavius held his breath until he had gone by. He was so thirsty, he could spit cotton. Moistening his mouth, he voiced one of many worries. "What if you get delayed? What if I should get there before you? They'll pick me off as sure as God made green apples."

"We'll reach the hill first. Trust me," Davy said with complete confidence.

Flavius's palms were growing slick. Crockett had not let him down yet, but there was a first time for everything.

To soothe his friend, Davy remarked, "It's the only way. Remember my motto."

"'Always be sure you're right, then go ahead,'" Flavius quoted. If he'd heard that once, he'd heard it a million times. Which was all well and good for Davy, who was as brave as any man who ever popped out of a woman's womb. Flavius had no shortage of courage himself, but by nature he was as jumpy as a cat in a room full of rocking chairs. Situations like this frazzled his nerves something awful.

David Thompson

The trail entered dense growth. John Kayne paused. "Here's where we part company. Take these." Pulling his flintlocks, he gave one to each of the others.

"We're grateful," Davy said sincerely.

With a nod, Kayne veered to the left, vanishing like a ghost amid the foliage. Davy smiled at Flavius, then veered to the right. Immediately he ducked low, darting from cover to cover.

Avoiding birds that might be scared into flight and squirrels that might chatter to high heaven, Davy looped toward the far side of the hill. He tried not to think of Flavius, alone, easy pickings.

Think of Rebecca, he told himself. She mattered most. That he did not know her was unimportant. It was his duty.

The woods thinned out again close to the side of the hill. Davy had to pick his route with extreme caution. Darting from boulder to log to tree to bush, he came to a narrow gully slashed out of the hill by erosion. It angled upward, affording ideal cover.

Having the pistol was a comfort, but Davy had no illusions about the outcome should he stumble on the entire war party. Whether he ever held his wife and kids in his arms again depended on how stealthy he could be. Avoiding dry twigs and grass, he hastened around a boulder. Shocked, he drew up short.

Six feet away stood an equally dumbfounded warrior painted for war and armed with a glittering lance.

Chapter Four

Honed by a lifetime of wilderness living, tempered by clashes with beasts and bloodthirsty men alike, Davy Crockett's reflexes were second to none.

So it was that when the dumbfounded warrior recovered his wits, lowered the metal tip of his long lance, and speared it at Davy's chest, Davy sidestepped and countered by slamming his pistol across the warrior's temple.

Firing a shot was out of the question. It would alert the rest of the war party to his presence, and leave him with an empty, useless weapon.

The Indian's knees buckled, but he did not go down. Shaking his head to clear it, the warrior swung viciously at Davy's midsection, the keen blade missing by a whisker. In spinning, the man exposed his side. Wedged under the cord that held up his breechclout was a tomahawk. Davy's *own* tomahawk.

David Thompson

In a flash Davy snatched it and brought the blunt end crashing down on top of the Indian's head. Like a disjointed puppet whose strings have been cut, the warrior sprawled forward and lay still.

Davy glanced up the gully. No other Indians were visible. Stooping, he dragged the warrior back around the huge boulder. Lacking rope, he stripped off the man's leggings and used the warrior's knife to cut them into strips. After binding the Indian's wrists and ankles and gagging him, Davy squatted.

How had his own tomahawk come to be in the man's possession? The only explanation Davy could think of was that it had been taken from one of the Sauks during the fight at the stream.

So now Davy had three weapons. Or did he? A hasty inspection of the pistol revealed that it was undamaged and primed to fire.

Davy resumed climbing. He exercised more stealth than ever before, his back to the gully wall in case he was jumped, ready to flee at a moment's notice if the main band appeared.

Davy neared the top of the hill. The gully narrowed to a jagged cleft that rose another ten feet. There was barely room for him to fit, but fit he did, squeezing in and climbing.

The going was arduous and unbearably slow. Grains of dirt trickled from under his moccasins, and once a tiny rock dislodged and fell with a muffed thud. But he reached the top unchallenged and poked his head up.

A grassy rectangle dotted with trees made for a parklike setting. Davy did not want to expose himself until he was confident unfriendly eyes were not observing him, so, clambering out, he crawled to an oak and cautiously eased onto his knees.

Somewhere a robin chirped. To the east flitted a

yellow and black butterfly. The aromatic fragrance of wildflowers filled the air.

It was so peaceful, so quiet, that Davy was inclined to think he had been wrong. The war party had no intention of springing an ambush. A single warrior had been left behind to watch the back trail, that was all.

Then someone coughed. Davy spun around, and off through the high grass he glimpsed a buckskin-clad form prone on the green grass. The man was gazing into the valley, no doubt at Flavius.

Like a panther stalking prey, Davy advanced. The knife remained in his sheath, the pistol tucked under his belt. For close-in, quiet work, he preferred the tomahawk.

The young warrior was dressed as the man in the gully had been: in a breechclout, leggings, and high moccasins. A shaggy mane of shoulder-length, raven hair was adorned with a single eagle feather. His cheeks and forearms were streaked with alternating bands of red and yellow paint.

The significance of the marks eluded Davy, as did the identity of the tribe the warrior belonged to. The Indian was taller than most, sinewy and whipcord tough.

At the last tree Davy halted. To reach his quarry he must cross a ten-foot open stretch. It would help if John Kayne were there to back him up, but there had been no sign of the settler. What was keeping him?

The Indian shifted, rising onto one knee. From beside him he lifted a bow. Strapped to his waist was a slender quiver packed with arrows. Sliding a shaft out, he nocked it to the sinew string and took aim at something below.

At Flavius, Davy feared. Throwing caution aside,

Davy charged. He fairly flew, yet even so, the warrior heard him and spun before he could strike. The arrow tip swiveled, aligning itself with his chest. He saw the bowstring jerk back.

Davy flung himself to the right just as the string twanged. The shaft whizzed past and thunked into the oak. Driving himself forward, Davy sprang, his blow missing the warrior but smashing the second arrow the man had drawn.

Snarling, the Indian hurled the shattered shaft at Davy's face, then vaulted erect and skipped to the left, putting distance between them in order to nock another arrow.

Davy could not allow that. Pouncing, he slashed at the warrior's wrist, but the Indian dodged aside. A swipe of the tomahawk nicked the ash bow but did not prevent the man from yanking out a third shaft and applying it to the string.

Another second and the warrior would let the arrow fly! Davy dived—and tripped! Jarring his elbows and knees, he looked up at the gleaming arrow tip and beyond it at the gleam of fierce triumph that lit the warrior's dark, smoldering eyes.

Davy saw one of those eyes explode outward, as if in slow motion. Along with it, part of the nose and cheek ruptured, spraying flesh and blood over the warrior's chest, over the grass, and over Davy. The blast of a rifle echoed off across the valley.

Pumping scarlet, the warrior swayed. The bow and arrow clattered at his feet. Somehow he was able to take a shambling step, then keeled over.

Davy straightened, wiping his face with a sleeve. On the far side of the hill stood John Kayne, smoke curling from the muzzle of the Kentucky rifle. Kayne waved and ran toward him.

No more Indians materialized. Davy stepped to the

edge but did not see Flavius. Plucking grass, he wiped bits and pieces of flesh off his buckskins. Blood smeared his left sleeve and his shoulder. He needed to take a dip in a stream soon, or before long he would stink worse than a polecat.

Kayne reloaded on the move. "You're lucky I showed when I did," he declared. "I'd have been here sooner, but the north side of this hill is a sheer cliff. Took me forever to climb."

Davy stripped the dead warrior of a knife, as well as the bow and quiver. "See any others?"

"No, but I crossed their trail. The main party headed northeast. None of Rebecca's tracks were mixed in with theirs, so she must still be on horseback." Kayne nudged the body with a toe. "It would help if we knew what tribe these jaspers are from, but I'm still stumped."

"Maybe our prisoner can shed some light," Davy said.

"You caught one?"

"See for yourself."

The warrior had his back to the gully and was doubled over a tooth-edged rock. Frantically rubbing the deerskin that bound his wrists, he had almost succeeded in slicing one of the strips in half.

"No, you don't, hoss," Davy said, pushing the man backward and kicking the rock. "You're going to answer some questions before we let you go."

Cradling his rifle, Kayne stabbed a finger at the warrior. "You can't be serious. The only good Indian is a dead Indian. If we let him live, he'll be back again someday to pillage and rape."

Davy hunkered facing the prisoner, who glared defiance. "Do you savvy English?" he asked. When that prompted no reply, he resorted to the Creek tongue. He wasn't fluent, but he knew enough to get by.

"Who are you? Where are you from?"

The warrior spat on him.

"See?" Kayne said. "There's no reasoning with these savages. Let's get going. Rebecca is more important."

"Hold on." Davy had another idea. Recently, while held captive by the Nadowessioux, or Dakotas, he had learned some of their finger talk, or sign language, as some called it. "Question?" he now signed. "You called?"

Comprehension animated the warrior. But with his wrists bound, the best he could do was wriggle his fingers.

"Cover him," Davy told Kayne. "I'm fixing to parley. Don't shoot unless he tries something."

"Sure you know what you're doing?" Kayne asked skeptically. Nonetheless, he backed up a few feet and leveled his rifle. The click of the hammer being cocked stiffened the warrior, who recoiled.

"We no harm you," Davy signed to put the man at ease. "I free you, but you sit still." Untying the knots took longer than he had anticipated. He had bound them so tight, he had to pick and pry for minutes on end. Once done, he slid backward to keep temptation, namely himself, out of the warrior's reach.

Sign language, Davy had learned, was wonderfully simple and logical, but it did have its drawbacks. For one thing, only the equivalent of what white men called nouns, adjectives, and verbs were used. The fine points of speech that his teacher had been so insistent every educated person must learn were missing.

So if he wanted to say, for instance, that "five boys are walking toward camp," in sign language that came out as, "Five boys walk camp." There were no signs for "are" or "toward."

As Davy had done in the Sioux village, he now did here. Mentally, he filled in the missing words as he went along, which made it easier for him to understand what the warrior was saying. "Question. How are you called?" he began.

"Thunder Heart," the warrior signed.

"What tribe do you belong to?"

The man's hands moved fluidly. Some of the signs Davy knew, others were new to him. But the gist of it, Davy felt, was "My people are known as the Men With Big Bellies."

Davy frowned. He must have misunderstood, so he tried again. The warrior repeated the same gestures, and Davy could not decide if they meant "Men With Big Bellies" or "Big Men with Bellies." Either made no sense, since neither Thunder Heart nor the man Kayne had shot was unusually big or had a big stomach. "Where are you from?"

Thunder Heart motioned vaguely north and west.

"How many suns did you travel to get here?"

The warrior did not answer.

"Why did you come?"

Again the warrior did not move a finger.

"We know that you have taken a white woman from bad Indians who stole her from her lodge," Davy signed as best he could. "We thank you for that. But now we want her back."

"No white woman," the man responded.

"Do not lie to us," Davy signed sternly. "Tracks do not lie. We want the woman. We want our horses. If you do not give them to us, we will follow your people to your own country and punish them."

The warrior's mouth quirked upward. "Three of you will do all this?"

Davy was tired of being played with. "Do not mock me," he warned. "My friends and I are scouts. We blaze a trail for a large party with many guns. Behind them are even more men with even more guns. Word is spreading throughout our country. Soon a hundred times a hundred men will be on the march, with others to come. We will not rest until our woman is safe or your people are destroyed."

Indecision etched the warrior's face. He glanced at the Kentucky rifle Kayne held, then at the pistol tucked under Davy's belt.

"If you know anything of the white man," Davy pressed on, "you know that we have more guns than there are birds in the air or fish in the rivers. You also know that we do not show mercy when our women have been wronged."

Thunder Heart gnawed his lower lip.

"If you come from the north, maybe you do not know the power of the white man. Maybe you do not know that our medicine is so strong, none have stood before us. The tribes who opposed us and are no more cannot be counted on all your fingers and toes."

Davy knew that he was stretching the facts, but it was necessary. Unless Thunder Heart's people were persuaded to return Rebecca Worthington, there would be hell to pay. The settlers would retaliate. "An eye for an eye, a tooth for a tooth" was the byword of the frontier. And if the settlers couldn't find the culprits, they'd make do with handy scapegoats. Innocents on both sides would pay for the stupidity of a few.

Davy held his right hand under his chin, close to his neck, fingers folded, then moved his index finger and thumb straight forward. In effect, he was signing, "I speak with a straight tongue."

The warrior was glum. "I believe you, white man," he responded. "But there is nothing I can do. The man who leads my band, He-Bear, has claimed the woman as his own. He will take her to our village and make her his wife."

"Even if it costs the lives of his people?"

"He-Bear cares only about He-Bear," Thunder Heart signed.

"But what of the other warriors? Surely they will not let one man bring the wrath of the whites down on your tribe?"

"They dare not challenge our leader," Thunder Heart said. "He-Bear would cast them out."

In exasperation, Davy threw up his arms and walked in a circle, thinking furiously. Few tribes were organized the same. In some, leaders held limited power, and their opinions mattered no more than those of a common warrior. In other tribes—and this, unfortunately, was one of them—the leaders' will was absolute; their word was law.

Davy stopped pacing. Maybe, where force and threats would not work, other incentives might. "Answer me this, Thunder Heart. And answer honestly." He locked eyes with the warrior. "Would you like to settle this without blood being shed?"

"I would," Thunder Heart signed earnestly.

Davy believed him. Just as all whites were not inveterate Indian-haters, not all Indians despised whites. Reason and tolerance could prevail if given the chance. "Question. Would He-Bear be willing to trade for the woman?"

"Trade what?"

Davy hesitated. He had no right to speak on the settlers' behalf. They might not be willing to keep any promises he made. "For whatever He-Bear wants," he hedged. "Horses, blankets, knives."

"He will want guns."

"That is not for me to decide."

"Guns," Thunder Heart insisted. "We took two from the men we fought. But we need many more to keep our enemies from our village."

On a hunch, Davy signed, "So that is why your band came south? Your tribe is at war, and the other side is winning. Without guns your people will lose."

Thunder Heart did not sign anything. He did not have to. His expression confirmed that Davy's guess had been right.

"If I let you go, will you tell He-Bear all that we have talked about? Will you tell him that we are willing to trade—" Davy breathed deep, "and we will give him guns, if that is what it takes?"

"I will tell him," Thunder Heart's bronzed hands declared.

Kneeling, Davy removed the gag and cut the strips wrapped around the warrior's ankles. "My friends and I will wait on top of this hill until tomorrow when the sun is directly overhead. If He-Bear accepts our offer, have him bring the woman. If he does not come, your people will suffer."

John Kayne had tensed when Davy freed the warrior. Now he extended his rifle, demanding, "What's going on, Crockett?"

"We're letting him go."

"Like hell we are!" Kayne said. "He's our ace in the hole. We'll swap him for Rebecca."

Unaware of what they were talking about, Thunder Heart nodded at Davy and started to walk off. Two steps he took, and Kayne thrust the rifle against his ribs.

"This buck isn't going anywhere," the settler insisted. "Tie him up and we'll wait for Norval and Cy to get here."

"I've made a deal," Davy said, and detailed his talk, concluding with "It's the best chance we have of averting more bloodshed. Besides, what harm can it do?"

"Plenty, if this red fiend and some of his pards decide to sneak back in the middle of the night and slit our throats," Kayne said.

"The others will join us by then. We'll post guards." Davy did not fault Kayne for being so reluctant. Few whites trusted the red man, just as few Indians had a high opinion of whites. "Please. For Rebecca's sake."

"I'd do anything for her," Kayne said. Wavering, he gave in and lowered the Kentucky. "I just pray that you know what you're doing," he puffed in annoyance.

Thunder Heart did not waste another second. As lithe as a cougar, he bounded to the east slope and was gone. He did not look back.

Davy could not help wondering if he had made one of the biggest mistakes of his life. He had put his trust in a warrior he did not know, from a tribe he had never heard of. How wise was that, with a woman's life hanging in the balance? If he had misjudged Thunder Heart, Rebecca Worthington would suffer the consequences.

"So what now, Tennessee?" Kayne asked.

"We wait."

They trudged to the top. Davy suggested they build a signal fire. Kayne moodily offered to collect wood. Presently flames licked the air a full yard off the ground and a sinuous plume of smoke spiraled high into the sky.

"There. They should see that from miles off," Davy predicted.

"Where's your friend?" Kayne asked.

Davy had not been overly worried until the question was posed. After all, they had advised Flavius to go slowly and stop every so often. And knowing his friend's aversion to combat, he had figured that Flavius would show up sooner or later.

But with the signal lit, and no sign of his companion, Davy grew disturbed. Moving to the edge, he cupped his hands to his mouth and hollered loud enough to be heard back in Tennessee. His shouts went unanswered.

Kayne added fuel to the fire. "He has to be all right," he said. "Otherwise, we would have heard a shot."

Maybe not, Davy mused, if Flavius had been jumped and overpowered before he could pull back the hammer and squeeze the trigger. "Stick with the fire and keep it high. I'm going to check on him."

"Keep your eyes skinned, hoss. Might be that those heathens have two captives instead of just one."

Praying that wasn't the case, Davy jumped, coiled, and jumped again. The slant of the slope enabled him to descend swiftly. At the bottom he hollered some more.

Four crows flapped skyward from the top of a tall tree. Nothing else moved. Darting into the woods, Davy angled to the game trail. Hoofprints and moccasin tracks made by the war party were abundant. Flavius's tracks should have been impressed on top of them, but they were missing.

Breaking into a sprint, Davy hurtled along the trail at a reckless pace. He did not chide himself for leaving Flavius alone. It had been the right thing to do. Even so, if anything had happened to the portly grump, he would never forgive himself.

Presently Davy slowed to examine the trail. He was two hundred yards from the hill, yet Flavius had not reached that point. Avoiding horse droppings, he paralleled the trail for another fifty feet. Suddenly he halted.

At last Davy had found some of Flavius's prints. Unaccountably, his friend had stopped and crouched, as the deep heels demonstrated. Then Flavius had turned and gone into the vegetation to the west.

Davy did likewise. He had brought the bow, and he nocked a shaft. As a boy he had used one many times, playing Robin Hood with his brothers and chums. But he was nowhere near as accurate with it as he was with a rifle.

The lush forest hemmed him in. Insects were everywhere: ants crawling at his feet, bees buzzing in search of pollen, flies doing whatever it was flies did when they weren't feasting on rotten carcasses.

To Davy, his friend's tracks were like an open book. They led him to a large log where Flavius had sunk to his knees. After crawling to the opposite end, Flavius had risen and dashed to a pine tree. At its base he had crouched, perhaps to scour the area ahead, perhaps to listen.

Flavius had gone on. Davy started to, then felt the short hairs at the nape of his neck prickle.

A new set of footprints converged on Flavius from behind a bush. Whoever it was had shadowed him, staying far enough back that Flavius never caught on.

Davy ran, anxious to learn the outcome.

In an oval clearing ringed by saplings Flavius had been set on by three men wearing moccasins. Flavius had put up quite a fight, but he was overpowered and borne to the earth. His attackers, though, had not slain him. It relieved Davy to discover that Flavius had walked off under his own power, surrounded by the trio.

David Thompson

The prints of the attackers raised more questions than they answered. Davy had seen the style of moccasin before. He even recognized one set because the right heel was split.

Flavius Harris had been taken captive by the same warriors who had kidnapped Rebecca Worthington.

Chapter Five

At that exact moment, the man Davy Crockett was worried about trudged gloomily through heavy brush. Whenever he slowed, the sharp tip of a long knife prodded him in the small of his back. "Keep jabbing me with that pigsticker, damn you," he grumbled after the fourth or fifth time, "and I'll take it from you and shove it down your throat."

The warrior holding the knife merely grunted and prodded him again.

Flavius blamed himself for being captured. If he had stuck to the trail as he was supposed to do, if he hadn't let curiosity get the better of him when he heard faint whispering, he wouldn't be in the pickle he was in.

It had surprised him immensely when the warriors made no attempt to slay him after they battered him to the ground and relieved him of the pistol. The tallest had hoisted him upright and shoved him into the woods, and they had been hurrying northward ever since.

In due course Flavius recognized them.

They were the same warriors who had attacked Davy and him the night before. Their leader was the tall warrior who favored a war club, and who now carried one of Davy's pistols. Behind Flavius tramped the stocky warrior who had wanted to slit Davy's throat. The third man carried a lance and one of Flavius's flintlocks, and had a wicked gash in his side. Of the other two pistols there was no sign.

What was it Norval had called them? Flavius asked himself. Sauks, or Sacs, as he recollected. He keenly desired to learn what they intended to do with him. As yet they had not bound him or harmed him in any way. And it was somewhat encouraging that the tall warrior had spared Davy when Davy was at their mercy.

Preoccupied, Flavius did not see a root in his path until his toe snagged it and he stumbled. Throwing his arms out, he managed to stay on his feet. But it earned him another prod.

"Damn you!" Flavius fumed, whirling with his fists clenched. "You're so dumb, you couldn't teach a hen to cluck! Didn't you see that root? I didn't trip on purpose."

The stocky Sauk glared, blood lust lining his brutal visage. He yearned to use his knife. That much was obvious.

The man's attitude just made Flavius madder. "I ought to pound your head in, you yak!" he declared, venting his frustration the only way he could.

For a second it appeared that the stocky warrior was going to cut him. Poised to slash, the man wagged his blade. Instantly, a tall figure glided between them.

Blood Hunt

At a command from the leader, the stocky Sauk lowered his arm and stepped back. The tall one turned, regarding Flavius wearily. "Keokuk will not harm you if you do not give us any trouble, white man. I give you my word."

Flabbergasted at hearing flawless English uttered by one of his captors, Flavius blurted, "You speak our tongue? Why didn't you say so sooner?"

"There was no need," the tall warrior responded, and gestured for Flavius to fall into step. "Now, come."

"Who are you? Why have you taken me captive? What's this all about?"

The warrior glanced back. He had a stately presence, accented by the turban-style headdress that framed his high forehead. His moccasins and leggings were finely decorated. Over his broad shoulders was draped a cloak of sorts, made from bear and otter. "Be quiet, white man. We must hurry if we are to take back the woman stolen by the Atsinas."

Gambling that the Sauks were not disposed to rub him out, Flavius paid no heed. "I need to know your name. And why I'm your prisoner."

"I am Pashipaho."

That was all the man would say. So Flavius tried again. "Why did you jump me? Where are you taking me? And how is it that you know the white man's language?"

"A missionary taught me," Pashipaho said.

"When?"

"When I had seen but six winters. He came among our people and taught us white ways, and about the white God, and of your Great Father who lives in a stone lodge far away." Pashipaho paused. "He was a kind man, Father McKenzie. My people thought highly of him."

"If that's so, why are your people trying to drive the whites out?

Without warning, Pashipaho halted, and Flavius nearly collided with him.

"The missionary did not take land that had belonged to my tribe since the world began," Pashipaho said harshly. "The missionary did not take all the fish from our streams and the game from our woods. The missionary did not make my people act foolish from drinking too much alcohol, and he did not try to force himself on our young women."

Flavius never had understood why Indians made such a fuss when whites moved into a new area. There was plenty of land for everybody. And white folks had to put food on the table, just like everyone else.

"We liked Father McKenzie," Pashipaho said. "We thought all whites were as he was. So when the first trappers and traders came, we did not object. Now we see that we were wrong. Your people can never live in harmony with mine. We should have driven them out when we had the chance."

"So you don't cotton to any of my kind," Flavius guessed.

Pashipaho averted his gaze. "I did not say that, white man. Were it true, you and the one who wears the tail of a raccoon on his head would now be with your ancestors."

They hiked on awhile, Flavius pondering how best to pry more information from the Sauk. He was surprised when Pashipaho addressed him first.

"I spent a lot of time among your people, white man. I visited the settlement every day for over a year. I thought that maybe our elders were wrong, that maybe all of us could live in peace." His voice dropped. "I should have known better."

"What happened?"

"What do you think? Some of the whites at Peoria came to me and shoved guns in my face and told me to leave and never return. So I left. But I could not stay away."

"How do you mean?"

Pashipaho looked around. "What is your name, white man?"

Flavius told him, adding, "My pard and me are from Tennessee, which is even farther away than the Great White Father's stone lodge. We're just passing through. We're no threat to you or yours."

"Well, Flavius Harris of Tennessee, I am sorry for what must be done. If I could, I would not do it. I do not believe in killing a man unless he tries to kill me."

"What's this talk of killing all of a sudden?" Flavius asked. "I told you we came in peace."

Pashipaho started to answer, then tilted his head and sniffed loudly. The other Sauks imitated him. Flavius tested the air but smelled nothing out of the ordinary. The next moment, the stocky warrior behind him pressed the knife against his throat and seized him by the scruff of the neck.

"From here on, follow me closely, white man," Pashipaho whispered. "Do not make any noise. If you do, you will make Keokuk very happy. Do you understand?"

Flavius understood perfectly. Keokuk was looking for any excuse to sever his jugular. Gulping, he cat-footed on Pashipaho's heels.

The Sauks were ghosts incarnate. They trod on air, or seemed to, for not one made the faintest sound. Bent low, they sped in a beeline toward an unknown destination.

Not until the acrid odor of smoke tingled Flavius's nose did he have a clue where they were going. He marveled that the warriors had smelled the campfire from twice the distance he could.

Muffled voices brought the Sauks to a stop. Dropping to their hands and knees, the warriors warily moved forward. Keokuk stayed close to Flavius, the knife conspicuously close to Flavius's chest. A short stroke, and cold steel would wind up in his heart.

A thicket screened them from a clearing in which a number of figures moved about. The Sauks flattened. Flavius hesitated, thinking that the people ahead might be white men. A yell from him would bring help. Keokuk disabused him of the notion by lightly jabbing his arm.

The warriors snaked into the thicket. Flavius saw the figures clearly and was glad he hadn't shouted.

They had found the war party from Canada.

Across the way were the sorrel and bay, tied to cottonwoods. Seated in a circle were five painted warriors. Two others were beside a narrow stream. The Atsinas, as Pashipaho had called them, were broad, sturdy, somber men. About half wore buckskin shirts. All were well armed, and among their weapons Flavius numbered his rifle and Davy's, as well as the two missing pistols.

A husky warrior with a moon face, whose left cheek bore a jagged scar, was talking in a tongue Flavius had never heard. He had an arrogant bearing, and was stroking Davy's rifle, which rested across his stout thighs.

But it was the lone figure near the horses that most interested Flavius. Slender hands bound behind her back, Rebecca Worthington knelt facing her captors. Grime caked her face and her disheveled golden hair was dampened by perspiration. Her dress had been torn in spots, her right shoulder exposed. Yet she knelt there in quiet dignity, her chin high, defiance radiating from every pore.

Flavius had seldom seen so lovely a female. He would never admit as much, but she had Matilda beat all hollow. Happening to glance at Pashipaho, he was perplexed to see the Sauk gazing at Rebecca with what could only be described as intense longing.

The two warriors by the stream joined their fellows. One said something that earned a stern rebuke from the large warrior with the scar. The leader, Flavius reckoned.

Pashipaho wiggled a finger and the three Sauks silently wormed backward. Flavius tried to be as quiet as they were. He drew a barbed look from Keokuk when he accidentally applied his weight to a dry twig that crunched under his knee.

All four of them froze, but none of the Canadian Indians had heard.

Retreating a dozen yards from the thicket, Pashipaho issued instructions in his own tongue to Keokuk, then whispered to Flavius, "I will go talk to He-Bear, leader of the Atsinas. You will do as Keokuk wants you to do while I am gone. Is that clear, man from Tennessee?"

Flavius wondered why the Sauk made it a point to stress where he was from. "I savvy, mister," he whispered. "I'll be a good boy. I'm partial to breathing."

A few last remarks to the Sauks, and Pashipaho left, circling to the right.

Wearing a sadistic grin, Keokuk jabbed Flavius with the knife, then pointed at the camp. Flavius retraced their steps and was guided into the thicket. Nothing had changed, except that all the Atsinas were seated.

That changed a minute later when out of the undergrowth came Pashipaho. Strolling along as if he did not have a care in the world, his spine straight, wide shoulders swaying, the Sauk slanted toward the war party.

The Atsinas leaped to their feet, many jabbering at once. At a roar from the scarred warrior, who Flavius surmised must be He-Bear, they quieted and spread out. Rifles, lances, and arrows were trained on the Sauk, who showed no fear.

Flavius figured they would converse in the funny finger talk Davy had learned among the Dakotas. Then he remembered that tribes living in the vicinity of the Great Lakes did not use sign language.

Pashipaho stopped and spoke in—of all things— English. "We meet again, He-Bear."

The big Atsina snorted like his namesake. "Pashipaho. I not think you so stupid. We almost kill once. Now you let us finish you." His accent on many of the words was atrocious, and he slurred them terribly.

Pashipaho extended the pistol that belonged to Crockett. "Yes, there are enough of you to slay me. But I will kill at least one before I drop. Guess which one it will be?"

Rumbling mirth cascaded from the Atsina chief. "Always sly, like fox. What you want, Sauk? Where other warriors?"

"I came alone," Pashipaho said.

"And I fly like bird," He-Bear retorted.

Flavius watched the other Atsinas, afraid they would fan into the woods to search for Sauks. He also saw Rebecca Worthington, wide-eyed, staring at Pashipaho in amazement. Amazement, and another emotion he could not quite peg.

"What you want, Sauk?" He-Bear asked. "You want guns back? Maybe next time you not put down when enemies near, eh? Or you want horses? Which?"

"I want the white woman."

He-Bear's bushy brows knit. Lumbering past the line of warriors, he held Davy's rifle out. "You want female, not this? Not bullets? Not powder?"

"The woman," Pashipaho said.

The Atsina acted like a grizzly confused by an unfamiliar scent. He walked a few steps to the right, then a few steps to the left, his moon of a head swinging ponderously from side to side. "Why this be, Sauk? What woman to you?"

"That is my concern, not yours," Pashipaho said. "I will give you two more pistols in exchange for her, and let you keep the guns and the horses you stole."

The terms provoked more gruff mirth. "You let us keep what we already have, eh?" He-Bear sobered and spat on the grass. "This what I think. We keep guns, we keep horses, we keep woman with golden hair."

Pashipaho had not lowered the flintlock. Casually taking a few steps to the left, which put him nearer Rebecca, he said, "What is she to you? Surely she is worth two pistols. The white man's weapons are not easy to come by."

Patting Davy's rifle, He-Bear said, "I have gun. As for woman, maybe she be wife. Maybe she be slave." A grin split the scarred moon. "Maybe she be dog."

Pashipaho took another step. "What if I have something else you want even more."

"What that be?" He-Bear sneered. "A hundred rifles? A hundred horses? Another white woman?"

"No. A white *man*."

Flavius was not sure he had heard correctly. Where was the Sauk going to get a white man to swap for Rebecca Worthington? A bolt of lightning seared him when he suddenly realized that Pashipaho meant *him*. "Oh, God," he breathed, and was poked in the side by Keokuk's ever-ready blade.

He-Bear pursed his thick lips. "Why I want white man more than white woman?"

"I have heard stories." Pashipaho moved a few more feet. Intentionally or not, he was now a single bound from the captive. "I know you hate whites. I know that many winters ago you made friends with a white trapper who taught you some of their tongue."

The Atsina leader scowled. "Him no friend. He claim so, but he hurt sister, steal horse."

"Which is why nothing pleases you more than to torture one of his race. You like to hear them scream."

"They weak, these whites," He-Bear said, and chuckled. "Most cry like babies." He appraised Rebecca Worthington a moment as if evaluating her worth. "Women weak too. Not last long when captive."

"So will you trade? Rebecca Worthington for the white man I have?"

He-Bear tried to pronounce Rebecca's name but could not say "Worthington" properly. To justify his failure, he said, "White words twist tongue."

Pashipaho casually moved one last time, placing himself in front of Rebecca. Flavius could not be sure, but it appeared that the Sauk whispered to her out of the corner of his mouth. To the Atsina leader, Pashipaho said, "Think of it. A white man to do with as you please. What do you say?"

"Where man at?"

"I will have him brought when you agree. Do I have your word?"

Resuming his ponderous pacing, He-Bear did not

immediately reply. At length he turned to a short Atsina and they conferred in secret.

Flavius was sorely tempted to make a run for it.
Once the Sauks handed him over to the war party,
he was as good as dead. But he dared not try, not
with Keokuk's knife pressed against his ribs.

The huddle had ended. Smiling, He-Bear pivoted.
"All right, Sauk. We trade. Give us white man, two
pistols. We give you woman."

Lowering the flintlock, Pashipaho called out in his
own language.

Flavius was helpless. He had to let Keokuk and the
other Sauk seize him by the arms and haul him from
the thicket. Locked in their iron grasp, he was hustled into the clearing. This was it, he figured. His
time had come.

"Only three of you, eh?" He-Bear said. "I thought
maybe many."

Pashipaho was not paying attention. Rebecca
Worthington said something to him that caused him
to vigorously shake his head.

He-Bear's smile grew wider. "So you not lie, Sauk.
Now give pistols."

"And we're free to go? With the woman?"

"Pistols," He-Bear said, snapping his fingers.

Pashipaho started to comply, but Rebecca said his
name loud enough for all to hear. Stopping, Pashipaho thrust his pistol at Keokuk, who accepted it and
walked toward He-Bear.

Even though the knife was gone from his ribs,
Flavius did not try to run. The Atsinas would drop
him in his tracks. Resigned to the inevitable, he saw
He-Bear switch Davy's rifle to the crook of an elbow
to free his hands for receiving the flintlocks.

"We will leave," Pashipaho announced. Gripping
Rebecca's elbow, he pulled her up and propelled her
swiftly toward the safety of the forest.

From out of the trees in front of them stepped an eighth warrior, an arrow notched to the string of his bow. Abruptly stopping, Pashipaho looked back at He-Bear just as the Atsina leader clasped both pistols. "You gave your word!" Pashipaho cried.

"We give you woman," He-Bear said, hefting the flintlocks. He cocked them. "Not say how long keep her." Snapping the guns up, he fired the left one at Keokuk at point-blank range. The stocky Sauk staggered, his sternum shattered by the ball, then pitched onto his hands and knees.

Venting a war whoop, the third Sauk rushed to his friend's rescue. Four shafts were embedded in his torso in half that many steps. Snarling, he made a supreme effort to reach He-Bear, but his knees buckled.

"No!" Pashipaho raged, and flung himself at the Atsinas. His war club arched overhead. The blow he planned never landed, though, because the eighth warrior let his arrow fly. It sheared into Pashipaho's right shoulder, spinning him around and dumping him on his knees. The club fell from nerveless fingers as other Atsinas rushed to surround him.

"Leave him alone!" Rebecca shouted, rushing to the fallen Sauk. "Don't you dare hurt him any more!" Boldly, she bent over his back to protect him from the lances and knives of the Atsinas.

In all the confusion, the Indians had forgotten about Flavius. Or so he hoped. Whirling, he covered a yard. The blast of the second pistol and a ball whistling past his head changed his mind.

"Where you go, white man?" He-Bear said, snickering. "We want you stay."

Three Atsinas enforced their leader's wish by ringing Flavius and pushing him to where Keokuk was doubled in anguish. Pashipaho and Rebecca were brought over, too. A burly warrior threw Pashipaho down, then kicked him.

He-Bear was enjoying himself. He strutted back and forth to the admiring hoots and laughter of his followers. Giving the pistols to the short one, he bent over Pashipaho. "You stupid trust me. We enemies, Sauk. I kill you. You kill me. Never change."

Pashipaho was in torment. Clutching his shoulder, he said, "I thought you were a man of honor. I was wrong."

"Only honor in coup." So saying, He-Bear slid a Green River knife from a beaded sheath. Pashipaho raised his left arm to defend himself, but He-Bear was not interested in him. Spinning, the Atsina chief sank the cold steel twice into Keokuk's back.

"Soon your turn," He-Bear said, leering at Pashipaho.

Flavius's skin crawled as he contemplated the ordeal he faced. It would be better to go down fighting than suffer for hours on end. Judging the distance to He-Bear, he was all set to leap when a new warrior arrived on the scene. Bursting from the woods, the newcomer jogged to the Atsina chief and talked excitedly for some time.

He-Bear ran a finger along his knife, then held the finger over Pashipaho so bloody drops fell on the Sauk's head. "You not only one want woman. Thunder Heart say whites trade many guns, many horses, many blankets." He licked his finger clean. "We go see them. Act like friends. We smile. We talk. Then—" He-Bear made a slashing motion across his throat.

Chapter Six

"It'll be a cold day in hell before I hand over guns to a pack of stinkin' Injuns!"

Curt nods and flinty looks confirmed the declaration by Cyrus. The majority of settlers were unwilling to abide by the offer Davy Crockett had made. So the Tennessean appealed to the two men who were inclined to go along with him. "Talk to them, Norval. You too, Kayne. They're your friends. Make them listen to reason."

The two men were seated apart from the others, who were gathered around the fire. Norval sighed and said, "They'd only tell us to go sit on a porcupine, I'm afraid. If those Big Bellies show up, Cy and the boys will make worm food of the whole lot."

"But I gave my word we'd trade," Davy stressed. "And isn't it best if we can work this out without losing more lives?"

John Kayne was cleaning his rifle. Pausing as he

inserted the ramrod, he said, "Too much water has gone over the dam, hoss. You're not from these parts. You haven't had to deal with these savages day in and day out. They've caused no end of grief."

"So you'll sit and do nothing when they pour lead into the Indians?"

"No. I'll help them."

Davy walked off before his temper flared. Nothing was going right. Absolutely nothing.

Take Flavius. Davy had tracked his friend and the three Sauks until darkness made it impossible. Noting landmarks, he had sped to the hill. The rest of the Peorians had arrived, and he'd asked them for help. Give him four men, he had said, and he would track Flavius by torchlight.

The settlers refused. Cy was not about to go traipsing off "after somebody who ain't even from our settlement."

Norval wouldn't leave, either, until his niece was returned alive and well.

Kayne was the only one who agreed to go, but once Davy told them about the deal he had made with the Big Bellies, Kayne bowed out. "My neighbors come first. They'll need me. I'm mighty sorry."

Davy was at his wit's end. He couldn't go after Flavius until daylight, which was when the war party would most likely appear. If he stayed to try and make peace between the two sides, he might never see Flavius again. If he went after his friend, the settlers and the Indians would be at each other's throats in no time.

What should he do?

Davy spied the sentry Norval had posted making a circuit of the crest. They were to take turns until dawn, then spring their trap.

The thought of being party to rank slaughter did

not sit well with him. It was his *word* that was at stake—his promise that the Big Bellies or whatever their real name was could come in peace and swap for the woman.

So what if he had given it to Indians? A man's word was his bond. Everyone knew that. Those who failed to keep their promises were branded as worthless and never trusted again.

Only politicians could routinely make false promises and get away with it. And then only because everyone knew that lying was their stock-in-trade.

Under an oak Davy stopped and leaned against the trunk. Weariness nipped at his brain like termites at wood. He had been on the go for so long, with so little food and even less rest, that he found it difficult to think clearly.

Fretting was pointless. As his father had impressed on him time and again, when a man had a job to do, he went out and did it. He didn't moan and groan. He didn't shrivel into a ball and cry. A true man confronted challenges head-on.

The Crocketts had always been fighters. A close-knit clan, their outlook on life was summed up by the family motto that Flavius liked to poke fun at: "Always be sure you're right, then go ahead."

Doing the right thing was not always easy. Sometimes it was downright unpopular. But Davy would not think to back down from doing as his conscience dictated.

The whisper of a footfall brought Davy around in a blur, his right hand dropping to his tomahawk.

A startled Norval Worthington stopped dead. "Lordy, Crockett! You're a two-legged cat. I didn't mean to spook you."

"What do you want?" Davy bluntly demanded.

"To chew the fat a little." The older man sank

cross-legged to the earth and set his rifle across his legs. "I don't want you to think poorly of the others. Deep down they're decent men. Were you in their boots, you'd feel the same."

"Would I?" Davy said. "I had my fill of spilling blood during the Creek War, Norval. Killing only leads to more killing. It never solves a thing." Sighing, he gazed at the twinkling stars. "I wish I may be shot if I ever let myself be roped into going to war again. It just isn't worth the cost."

Norval plucked a blade of grass and stuck an end in his mouth. "You're right smart for a pup your age. Cyrus is of the opinion that you have a puny thinker, which is a case of the pot calling the kettle black if ever there was one."

"You see I'm right, then, don't you?"

"Hell, yes. But there ain't nothing I can do. Cy and the boys have been looking to pay the Indians back for a long time. This is their chance."

"What do they plan to do?"

"Half of us will hide. At the right moment, Cy will give a signal." Norval chewed on the grass. "That will be the end of that."

A sense of sadness came over Davy. Sadness at the stupidity of it all. "No, it won't end. Killing them will start a whole new round of bloodshed. Their people will want revenge, and butcher some of us. Then we'll slaughter some of them. And so on and so on until everyone forgets why the fighting ever started."

"Sentimental soul, ain't you?"

"All I'm saying," Davy responded, "is why resort to a gun when we can talk our differences out?"

Norval chuckled. "You've missed your calling, son. Any man who thinks like you do should go into politics. It's the only line of work where a feller can be a windbag and get paid for it."

Davy got back to the issue at hand. "Can you convince Cyrus to let me talk to the Indians before anyone shoots? Maybe they'll turn over your niece without a fuss."

Norval spat out the grass. "I'd only be wasting my breath. I know that boy. He's snake-mean through and through."

"Yet your brother wants him for a son-in-law?"

"My brother worships money. He always wanted to be rich but never had more than a hundred dollars to his name at any one time." Norval glanced toward the fire. "Well, now he's found a way."

"He's selling his daughter to the highest bidder. And you're letting it happen."

"What choice do I have? I can't rightly meddle in his business, now can I?" Norval bowed his head. "Festus and I never have seen eye to eye. He was the youngest, and my ma babied him so much that he grew up thinking the world should treat him the same way."

Davy had known people like that. They were so wrapped up in themselves, they never seemed to notice the misery they caused everyone else. "I feel sorry for your niece, and I don't even know her."

"She's the prettiest filly in these parts," Norval bragged fondly. "The sweetest woman you'd ever want to meet. Never has a cruel word for anyone." His body gave a slight shudder. "Pairing her with Cy is the same as consigning her to a living hell for the rest of her days."

"Why doesn't Festus's wife do something about it?"

"He'd beat her silly. She's had more black eyes than you could count."

They fell silent. Davy found himself longing for his family, for the comfort of his wife's embrace and the joy of bouncing their youngest on his knee.

Blood Hunt

Polly, his first wife, had been the gentlest, daintiest female ever born. And the most patient. Without complaint, she had always looked after their three children when he went off exploring or on hunting trips and later to war against the Creeks.

Losing her had nearly broken him. To sit by her bedside, holding a hand so weak she could not close her fingers, and see her suffering for hours on end, had been too much to bear. Her passing left him with three children to care for, the youngest an infant daughter.

He had not stayed a widower long. In the neighborhood lived a widow whose husband had been killed by the Creeks. They found solace in each other's company, and in time love had blossomed.

Now, sitting under a windblown oak on the hilltop deep in the wilderness, Davy missed Elizabeth so much that he almost vowed never to leave her again. Almost, but at the last moment he couldn't bring himself to do it. As much as he adored her—and he truly did—he could never give up his gallivants, never stop going off to see new country, to learn what lay over the next horizon.

Such thoughts occupied him for a while after he curled up close to the fire to keep warm. None of the settlers had a blanket to share; they didn't even have blankets for themselves. They had lit out after Rebecca's abductors thinking they would overtake the Sauks quickly.

Exhaustion enabled Davy to sleep soundly once he drifted off. He was awakened by the squawk of a jay shortly before sunrise.

Half the men were up already, a few stamping their feet and clapping their arms against the morning chill. Davy saw Cyrus over by a bush and went up to him. "Morning."

"Go away."

"We need to talk."

The stocky settler scratched the stubble on his chin. "There's nothin' I have to say to you, mister. You're an outsider here."

"It's about the Big Bellies—" Davy began.

Cy held up a hand. "Don't your ears work?" His upper lip curled in contempt. "I know what you've been up to. How you tried to get my uncle to stop us from doing what we're fixin' to do."

"It's wrong."

Anger blazed in Cy's eyes. "When did you become the Almighty, red-cheeks? Who are you to tell us what's right and what ain't? Go back to Tennessee where you belong and let us deal with our problems as we see fit."

Davy tried one last time. "If Rebecca hasn't been harmed, if we can get her back without a fight, why kill them?"

Cyrus gazed over Davy's shoulder. "Ever hear such a dumb question in all your born days, Dilbert?"

The weasel had approached unheard. Snickering in disdain, he said, "Sure haven't. Makes a body wonder how the folks down to Tennessee ever licked those Creeks."

It was hopeless. Davy turned to go, but Cy had more to say.

"Don't think of sneakin' off to warn those vermin, Crockett. You're to stay here until they come. And to make sure you do, Dilbert is goin' to keep you company." Cy bared his teeth. "Whether you like it or not."

The Irish in Davy flared into immediate fury. He took a step, intending to grab the settler by the shirt and shake him until his teeth rattled. Suddenly he became aware that several others had converged.

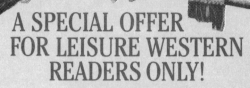

A SPECIAL OFFER FOR LEISURE WESTERN READERS ONLY!

Get FOUR FREE Western Novels

Travel to the Old West in all its glory
and drama—without leaving your home!

**Plus, you'll save between $3.00 and $6.00
every time you buy!**

GET YOUR 4 FREE BOOKS NOW—
A VALUE BETWEEN $16 AND $20
Mail the Free Book Certificate Today!

FREE BOOKS CERTIFICATE!

YES! I want to subscribe to the Leisure Western Book Club. Please send my 4 FREE BOOKS. Then, each month, I'll receive the four newest Leisure Western Selections to preview FREE for 10 days. If I decide to keep them, I will pay the Special Members Only discounted price of just $3.36 each, a total of $13.44. This saves me between $3 and $6 off the bookstore price. There are no shipping, handling or other charges. There is no minimum number of books I must buy and I may cancel the program at any time. In any case, the 4 FREE BOOKS are mine to keep—at a value of between $17 and $20! Offer valid only in the USA.

Name_____

Address_____

City_____ State_____

Zip_____ Phone_____

Biggest Savings Offer!

For those of you who would like to pay us in advance by check or credit card—we've got an even bigger savings in mind. Interested? Check here. ☐

If under 18, parent or guardian must sign.
Terms, prices and conditions subject to change. Subscription subject to acceptance. Leisure Books reserves the right to reject any order or cancel any subscription.

GET FOUR BOOKS TOTALLY *FREE*—A VALUE BETWEEN $16 AND $20

▼ Tear here and mail your FREE book card today! ▼

PLEASE RUSH
MY FOUR FREE
BOOKS TO ME
RIGHT AWAY!

Leisure Western Book Club
P.O. Box 6613
Edison, NJ 08818-6613

AFFIX
STAMP
HERE

"I wouldn't if I were you," Dilbert taunted.

Cyrus cockily put his hands on his hips. "Maybe we should truss him up, boys, until this is done. No tellin' what he might do otherwise."

There was a commotion. More of the rescue party had drifted over, including Norval, who draped a hand on the Tennessean's shoulder, declaring, "There's no call to bind him, Cy. That wouldn't be fitting."

"I don't trust him," countered Cyrus.

"Me neither," Dilbert piped up.

"What should we use?" asked another. "Since we don't have any rope, how about if we cut his hunting shirt into strips?" He drew his knife.

The settlers edged forward. Davy surreptitiously wrapped a hand around his tomahawk. Under no circumstances was he going to let them tie him up.

Tension crackled in the air. Cy, Dilbert, and a few others were on the verge of pouncing when John Kayne shoved to the forefront. "Enough," he told them. "Go about your business."

To Davy's surprise, they did just that. No one objected. No one even grumbled. Cy cast a hateful look at him but dutifully filed off with the rest. When all of them except Norval were gone, Kayne walked away without another word.

Davy did not know what to make of Kayne's intervention. Last night the man had made it clear he was going to help the others wipe out the Indians. Yet on his behalf, Kayne had bucked his own friends. "Why are they so scared of him?" he mused aloud.

"Kayne is one feller you don't want to cross," Norval said. "He's a quiet, peaceable man, until he's riled." He lowered his voice. "About two years ago, four 'breeds got rowdy in the settlement. They drank too much, and one of them slapped a girl who wouldn't let him kiss her. Kayne happened by and told them to leave."

Dilbert, Davy noticed, had not gone very far, and was watching him on the sly.

"Well, one thing led to another," Norval detailed. "The 'breed who had slapped the girl made the mistake of slapping Kayne, and Kayne knocked him down. So the four went for their knives."

"Did you see it happen?"

"I wish to God I did. They say it was the grandpappy of all knife fights. Those 'breeds were like berserk wolves, hacking and stabbing." Norval stopped. "Kayne killed all four without hardly working up a sweat. Ever since, ain't a man among us who will go up against him."

Over by the fire, Cyrus was beckoning. "Everyone! Gather around! The sun is rising! We have to get set for our visitors."

Davy moved to join them, but Dilbert barred his path. "Not you, Tennessee," he said. "This is just for us locals."

Only by a monumental effort of willpower did Davy keep himself from punching the weasel in the mouth. To remove the temptation, he turned on his heel and walked to the brink of the south slope.

Damn them to hell! Davy fumed, feeling his rosy cheeks flush redder. He had done what he could. Whatever befell them was on their shoulders, not his.

Besides, he had Flavius to think of. It had struck him as odd yesterday that the Sauk trail had paralleled the trail of the war party from Canada. What were the Sauks after? Revenge? Then why hadn't they gone to their village and brought reinforcements? The three of them could hardly expect to do much against a war party that size.

It was also peculiar that the Sauks had not harmed

Flavius. He was glad, mind, but he was also suspicious. What motive did they have? If they were going to kill Flavius, why hadn't they done it when they jumped him?

Davy's reflection was brought to an end by the arrival of the sentry, a man named Wilkins, who rushed from the north, yelling, "They're here! They're here!"

Davy ran to the fire. Wilkins had been surrounded by his excited companions and was being besieged by questions. A roar from Cyrus quieted them.

"Hush, you jackasses! Let the man talk!"

"They're about half a mile off," Wilkins reported. "I saw them as clear as day, crossing a clearing. They have Rebecca with them, too."

"Are you sure?" Norval asked anxiously.

"I couldn't mistake that blond hair of hers," Wilkins said. "They've brung her, just like Crockett said they would."

"So what?" Cyrus snapped. "That doesn't change anything. All of you know what to do. Get into position, and we'll give these heathens the shock of their stinkin' lives."

Four of the five settlers dashed to different oaks and commenced to shimmy up them with the agility of young black bears. Cyrus stood east of the dwindling fire, while Norval, Kayne, Dilbert, and Hillman fanned out in a horseshoe shape on either side of him.

The trap was cunningly laid. Since the north slope was too sheer to climb and the west slope too open, the Big Bellies would probably swing to the east, where the bushy slope afforded cover, or else come up the gully.

Once on top, the Indians would cautiously approach the camp. When they saw the whites out in the open, they would be reassured and expose themselves. They would enter the horseshoe, and at Cy's signal, the settlers would open fire. The men in the trees guaranteed that not one member of the war party would get away.

Davy was off to one side. He had the bow, his tomahawk, a knife, and the pistol Kayne had lent him, so he could defend himself if set upon. But he was not going to take part in the massacre. Not if he could help it, anyway.

The sun was perched on the eastern horizon, bathing the virgin wilderness in a golden glow. A hawk soared high overhead. Down in the valley a herd of deer browsed. The tranquil scene belied the volcanic carnage soon to be wrought.

For the longest while the rescuers waited, Cyrus and Dilbert impatiently fidgeting. The men in the trees had climbed high enough to be completely hidden by branches. Davy looked but did not detect them. Neither would the Big Bellies.

Rustling grass heralded the arrival of the war party. Into view stepped a brawny warrior, painted face inscrutable, armed with a bow. After studying the whites and the western portion of the hill, he tilted his head and yipped in perfect imitation of a coyote.

Three more Indians appeared as if up out of the very ground. One was an exceptionally big man whose face bore a scar. At a nod from him, the quartet slowly advanced, walking shoulder to shoulder.

Cyrus glanced at John Kayne. "I just had a thought. How the devil are we supposed to communicate with these stupid savages? Do you know any of that hand talk some tribes use?"

Davy was about to volunteer his services when the big Indian with the scar stopped shy of the horseshoe and announced in a booming voice, "I speak white tongue."

"You do?" Cy said, taken aback. "Well, that'll make it easier, I reckon. Not too many heathens are smart enough to savvy our language."

The big warrior did not like being insulted. "Only one white know ours," he countered.

Cy bristled. "Are you sayin' white men are dumber than your kind, Injun?"

"What you think?" the warrior rejoined, and straightened. "I be He-Bear."

Incensed, Cyrus gripped his rifle with both hands and took several steps. "I wouldn't care if you were Pocahontas. Mind what you say, or else!"

Norval clasped Cy by the wrist to restrain him. "Calm down, boy. Remember why we're here. First things first."

"What?" Cy said, so mad that he made as if to tear loose, then caught himself. "Oh. That's right. Sorry." Inhaling deeply, he stated, "All right, Injun. Where's Rebecca Worthington?"

He-Bear made a show of surveying the top of the hill from end to end. "Where guns? Where horses? I told you want trade. But nothing trade with."

"You didn't think we'd have it with us, did you? How do we know that we can trust you?" Cyrus craftily responded. "It's close by, though. All I have to do is give a signal and the stuff will be brought up from the valley. First, show me the woman is safe."

"How I know we trust you?" He-Bear said.

Cyrus blatantly smirked. "That's just the chance you'll have to take. Now quit stallin', Injun. Produce Rebecca so we can get this over with."

Davy expected He-Bear to be upset by the state of affairs. But the warrior grinned, more amused than anything else.

David Thompson

"You want woman? I show woman. And surprise."

"What kind of surprise?" Cyrus demanded.

The Big Belly leader raised an arm. Forty feet away a fifth Indian rose, wagging a pistol. Three more figures uncoiled. Rebecca Worthington was on the left. The tall Sauk Davy had tangled with was on the right. And in the middle, bound and gagged like the other two, was Flavius Harris.

As Davy looked on, the warrior placed the pistol's muzzle against the back of his friend's head.

"Try trick us," He-Bear warned, "and white man die."

Chapter Seven

Impulsively, Davy Crockett took a few steps, stopping only when a warrior next to He-Bear shifted and swung the glittering tip of a lance in his direction.

The Big Bellies' leader wore the look of a card player who held a winning hand. But unknown to He-Bear, Cyrus didn't give a damn what happened to Flavius or the Sauk. The only one Cy cared about was Rebecca Worthington.

"Bring guns plenty quick," He-Bear commanded. "We give white man. We give white woman. And Pashipaho, Sauk who take her."

Cyrus glanced at the tall Sauk. "So that's the bastard who caused us all this grief?" he commented, more to himself than for the benefit of anyone else. "You've done us a favor, He-Bear."

"I know," the Big Belly responded. "So fetch guns, eh? Horses, eh?"

"Sure, sure," Cy said. Turning, he moved to the

edge of the slope, cupped a hand to his mouth, and shouted, "Bring up the pack animals, boys! We've struck a bargain!" Strolling back, he told He-Bear, "See, Big Belly? The rifles and stuff will be here directly."

It was a ploy, Davy knew, to gain a little extra time and put the Indians more off their guard.

"Good," the big warrior grunted, then tapped his chest. "But we Atsinas. Not Big Bellies. That name French give."

"Whatever," Cyrus said, shrugging. He glanced meaningfully at Dilbert and Hillman. They began to slowly sidle to the right so they could shoot without running the risk of hitting Norval and Kayne, who were directly across from them.

Davy looked at Flavius. His friend was scared, but who wouldn't be?

In truth, Flavius Harris was more than scared. He was terrified. When he saw the Irishman stare at him, he arched his eyebrows and gave a barely perceptible jerk of his head to one side, striving to warn his friend about what was to come.

The movement puzzled Davy. He gathered that Flavius was trying to tell him something, but what? He motioned to show that he did not understand.

Flavius pushed against the gag with his tongue, but it had been wedged tight. Again he bobbed his head. He had to make Davy comprehend or they were all dead! Suddenly the warrior behind him snarled in the Atsina tongue and rapped him lightly with the pistol.

Davy wondered if perhaps his friend had spotted one of the men in the trees. Maybe Flavius thought he did not know about them.

He-Bear was talking in a relaxed manner, as if his suspicions were allayed now that the rifles and horses were being brought. "You smart, white man," he complimented Cyrus. "Not like most. Not shoot first, talk later. Soon you have woman. Have man. Do what want with Sauk."

Cyrus did not reply. His right hand strayed closer to the hammer of his rifle, which was cradled loosely in his left arm.

"Atsinas good Indians," He-Bear went on blithely. "Atsinas not kill woman. Not kill white man. We friends all whites. We do what right."

It occurred to Davy that He-Bear was rambling on for no apparent purpose. Almost as if the Atsina were stalling. He scrutinized the other warriors, who seemed a trifle too smug under the circumstances.

The next moment, with the force of a thunderclap, insight ripped through Dave, jangling every nerve in his body. *Where were the rest of the Atsinas?* He had counted eleven sets of prints at the stream. Later he had slain one. That left ten. But only five were there now. *Where were the other five?*

Davy looked at Flavius. Was that what his friend had been trying to tell him? Were the Atsinas going to spring a nasty surprise of their own? The settlers had to be warned. Taking a casual step, he whispered, "Cy!"

"Not now, Crockett," the hothead declared. "We're seein' this through. Interfere, and so help me God, I'll shoot you dead."

"But—" Davy began.

Cyrus was not listening. Plastering a fake smile on his face, he extended his right hand and asked He-Bear, "Can you snap your fingers, Injun?"

The Atsina leader was as perplexed as Davy. What did that have to do with anything? Then he knew. It was the signal. When Cyrus snapped his fingers, the settlers would attack. "Cy! Please listen!"

Cyrus ignored him. "Can you or not, heathen?" he baited his enemy.

"What 'snap fingers'?" He-Bear said.

"Here. I'll show you," Cyrus grandly offered, and elevating his arm, he snapped his.

There was nothing Davy could do. Dilbert and Hillman were watching him to ensure he did not meddle. Cyrus gave the signal; instantly the hilltop crackled with gunfire and lusty yells. But things did not work out as the whites had planned.

He-Bear must have sensed that something was amiss. For even as Cyrus snapped his fingers, He-Bear gave a signal of his own. Bounding to the left, the Atsina howled like a rabid wolf. It was the cue for his warriors to close with the whites, as from scattered points on the hill five hidden warriors leaped to their feet and charged.

All hell broke loose.

Guns boomed. Arrows whizzed. Heavy lances cleaved the air. White men and red men grappled in life-or-death struggles. Blood and oaths flew fast and furious.

In the midst of the bedlam, Davy Crockett sped toward his friend. He saw the warrior behind Flavius cock the pistol and prepare to blow Flavius's brains out. Davy brought up his own gun, but before he could fire a rifle thundered high in a tree and the warrior was catapulted backward by a heavy ball that smashed into his forehead.

Davy skirted Dilbert, who was locked in fierce combat with a husky Atsina. Hillman was already down, a lance jutting from his chest. Davy leaped over him, avoided another pair of fighters, and broke for the grass.

Flavius had ducked to keep from being hit by stray lead. He swiveled to see if the woman had done the same and was flabbergasted to find her sneaking off on the heels of Pashipaho. She was being foolish. A moving target always drew more fire.

Darting over, Flavius shouldered her aside. She spun, levering a leg to kick, a leg she lowered when she saw who it was. She gave him the oddest look.

Flavius nodded at the ground and squatted. To his amazement, she kept on going. *No!* he wanted to shout, but couldn't with the buckskin crammed into his mouth.

A ball thudded into the soil a few yards away. The next one might rip through the blonde.

Flavius jumped and tucked, bowling her over. Rebecca tumbled, winding up on her side with him across her legs. He had no intention of moving, even when she thrashed and squirmed and railed into her gag. They were safer where they were.

Davy was witness to his friend's heroic act. He was almost there when a painted visage reared before him and he stared down the muzzle of a rifle. Flavius's rifle, in the hands of an Atsina.

In pure reflex, Davy threw himself to the right. The Kentucky went off almost in his ear. Acrid smoke enveloped him as he rose to his knees, his ear ringing unbearably. A shape loomed, distorted by the smoke. He pivoted on the balls of his feet as the stock of Flavius's rifle swished past his head.

Davy rammed his pistol up and in. The muzzle gouged into firm flesh, and he fired. A yelp greeted the muffled retort. Diving clear of the smoke, he palmed his tomahawk.

The Atsina was still on his feet, one hand pressed over the wound in his belly, the other clawing for a knife. He had dropped the rifle. Ablaze with a thirst for revenge, he cleared the beaded scabbard, and thrust.

A deft arc of Davy's tomahawk parried the blow. Reversing his swing, Davy sheered into the man's chest. The warrior screeched like an enraged hawk and tried to sever Davy's neck, but Davy dodged, sidestepped, and brought the bloody edge of the tomahawk down on the crown of the Atsina's head.

All around, the battle swirled. Whites and Indians were prone, never to rise again. Puddles of blood stained the soil. Scarlet drops had spattered the grass.

Davy wrenched the tomahawk loose, claimed the rifle, stripped off the ammo pouch and powder horn, and ran to where Flavius lay on top of Rebecca Worthington. "I'll have you free in two shakes of a lamb's tail," he said, hunkering.

"I tried to warn you," Flavius said the second his gag was yanked out. Twisting so Davy could cut the strips that bound his wrists, he glanced up in time to see a settler pitch from a tree, the feathered end of an arrow protruding from the man's back. "Hurry!"

Davy worked as rapidly as possible. Shoving the rifle, ammo pouch, and powder horn at Flavius, he bent over the woman, who was gazing forlornly southward, not at the conflict. "We'll get you to safety, ma'am," he promised.

Rebecca did not respond or move. She appeared to be in the grip of sorrow so profound, she was blind to what was going on around her.

Davy pulled the woman to her feet and had to loop an arm around her waist to keep her from falling. "Are you hurt, Miss Worthington?" he asked. Receiving a blank gaze, he shook her gently. "Ma'am? Snap out of it. We're liable to be turned into pincushions if we don't make ourselves scarce."

"Where is he?" Rebecca said softly.

Blood Hunt

Thinking she might be referring to Cyrus or possibly Norval, Davy glanced over a shoulder. The hilltop was a madhouse of butchery and bloodshed. Neither was anywhere to be seen. Davy prayed that Norval had not been a casualty. As for Cyrus, he couldn't care less. He ushered her toward the gully. "We'd best light a shuck while we can."

"No!" Rebecca said. She tried to break loose.

The ordeal had sapped her energy. Davy had no problem pinning her arms to her sides as he swiftly steered her among the trees.

Flavius followed, reloading as he ran. He was in dire dread that the Atsinas would give chase at any moment. None did, though, and gradually the curses, screams, and clang of steel grew fainter.

They entered the gully, flying now, Davy supporting the woman, who had stopped resisting and was as limp as a wet rag.

Davy remembered seeing Thunder Heart in the thick of the clash, and resolved never to trust another Atsina for as long as he lived. The treacherous band never had any intention of trading for their captive. They were as bad as the settlers. Good riddance to the lot!

At least the woman had been saved. And Flavius was all right.

Davy looked back several times. Evidently none of the warriors had observed their escape. Reaching the bottom, he hustled into the trees.

Since Rebecca was having difficulty walking, and was as pale as a sheet, Davy stopped in deep shadow at the base of an oak and carefully lowered her so she could sit. "What's wrong, ma'am?" he tried again, worried that she had been violated. The shock of being outraged sometimes did terrible things to women.

"He's gone," she said.

"Who is? Cyrus? Your uncle?" Davy stroked her hair. "Maybe they got away," he suggested, although he very much doubted it.

Flavius did not say a word. He had a sneaking hunch why the woman was so distraught, but he kept it to himself for the time being.

Davy leaned Rebecca against the bole. "Why don't you rest a minute?" he said, even though they could not spare five seconds, let alone sixty.

Rebecca's lovely eyes focused on his face. Some semblance of life animated her countenance. "I'm sorry. I have no right to put your lives in danger. Let's go while we can."

Above them war whoops resounded. Davy crouched in front of her, unlimbering his tomahawk. Somewhere or other he had dropped the bow and not even realized it. Kayne's pistol was wedged under his belt, but he had not reloaded it.

Flavius sank behind a scraggy bush. It had not escaped his notice how He-Bear looked at the woman when she was not aware. The Atsina chief was not going to let her slip through his fingers.

Pebbles clattered in the gully, punctuated by the pad of moccasins. Several Atsinas appeared, one covered with blood not his own. They paused, staring right and left.

Three more Big Bellies appeared, one limping. It was He-Bear himself, a gash on his left thigh where a knife had bitten almost to the bone. His contorted face testified to his temperament. All the Atsinas carried rifles now, Davy saw, which could only mean one thing. He-Bear barked orders and the band spread out, racing into the trees like a pack of bloodhounds, heads bent to search for sign.

The Atsinas never suspected that their quarry was

only twenty feet from the gully mouth. And by a sheer fluke, none came within ten feet of the oak tree. Davy thought for sure that one of them was bound to spot the fresh tracks, but Fate smiled on him. The warriors melted into the forest, He-Bear last, hopping like an oversized jackrabbit.

"Whew!" Flavius exhaled when the Indians were gone. "If this day doesn't turn my hair gray, nothing will."

Davy warily stood. Sooner or later the Atsinas would backtrack. He had to have the woman long gone by then. But first there was an unpleasant duty to perform. "Stay with Rebecca," he told Flavius. "I'm going back up."

"What the hell for?"

"To find out if any of them are still alive," Davy said.

Flavius balked at being separated again. "You're wasting your time. Those red devils wouldn't have left, otherwise."

"We have to be sure. It's the right thing to do."

A mild oath escaped Flavius. "You and your conscience! One of these times, that hankering of yours to always do right will get you into more trouble than you can handle."

"Probably. But I have it to do." Davy started off, stopping when Rebecca asked him to wait. She rose, her temporary weakness gone.

"Take us with you."

"I don't know if that's wise," Davy hedged. Some of the Atsinas just might still be up on the hill. "You're better off here."

"I insist," Rebecca said, walking over to him. "Those men up there came on my account. They fought to save me. It's only right that I do what I can for them."

Flavius shook his head, muttering, "Lordy, there are two of you!"

Time was precious. Davy took the lead, leaving his friend to guard their rear. Smears of blood on the gully floor marked where He-Bear had walked. Shy of the rim, Davy guided Rebecca into a cleft. "Stay put until I've made certain the coast is clear."

"I'm not a little girl. I can take care of myself."

"Please," Davy said. "Flavius will watch over you." Climbing the rest of the way, he poked his head up high enough to survey the top. Fluttering leaves and rustling blades lent motion to a supremely tranquil scene. No one would ever guess that five minutes ago human beings had been killing each another in wanton abandon.

Rather than stand and expose himself, Davy slid to the west on his stomach, propelled by his elbows and knees. At the nearest tree he stopped and knelt. A smoky odor lingered in the air. Mingled with it was the unmistakable scent of freshly spilled blood. An aura of death hung heavily over the woodland.

The body of a dead settler was the first Davy spotted. The man had been speared low in the gut by a lance. To finish him off, his adversary had cut his throat. A pool of drying blood framed his head and shoulders in a scarlet halo.

Davy crept on by. Here and there were other bodies, mostly those of whites. Horror, shock, astonishment, dismay; the emotions portrayed in their contorted faces ran the gamut of reactions to dying.

Davy went to each and every one, checking for a heartbeat if it was not apparent that the victim had perished. He had confirmed five kills and was nearing a sixth form when a low groan gave him cause to hope.

Blood Hunt

It was a skinny man, on his stomach. Davy had to roll him over. "Dilbert!" he exclaimed.

The weasel had been transfixed by an arrow high in the left shoulder. In addition, his cheek had been slashed and his left wrist partially severed. The worst of all his wounds, however, was the one across his midsection. Someone had disemboweled him, leaving his intestines to spill out.

The stench was revolting. Covering his mouth, Davy moved on. Obviously, Dilbert had not been the one who groaned. Rounding a tree, he nearly stumbled over a middle-aged settler by the name of Craig, who had taken a ball in the ribs.

Placing a hand under the man's shoulders, Davy raised him high enough to prop against his left leg. "Craig?" he said. "Can you hear me?"

The settler's eyelids fluttered open. He gazed blankly at the sky, then blinked and licked his lips, which were flecked with red drops. "Kayne? That you? Everything is a blur."

Davy identified himself.

"One of the coons from Tennessee? Did we lick 'em, boy? Did we give 'em what for?"

What should he say? Davy reflected, surveying the bodies strewn pell-mell from the north end of the hill to the south. "We gave as good as we got" was his reply.

"Good." A contented smile creased Craig's weathered visage, a smile that died when he erupted in a violent coughing fit. He wheezed, grasped Davy's arm, and died. Just like that.

"Damn," Davy said softly. Lowering the body, he closed the man's eyes. He would have liked to dig a grave, but it was out of the question.

A twig cracked to his rear. In a twinkling Davy whirled, raised his tomahawk to throw. He scared

Rebecca so badly that she stepped back, a hand to her slender throat.

"It's only me!"

"I told you to wait in the gully," Davy said more gruffly than he intended. Beyond her, Flavius sheepishly pretended to be interested in a thistle. "You shouldn't have let her come."

"How was I to stop her?" Flavius protested. He'd objected when she tramped off, but short of throwing her to the ground and sitting on her, he had been powerless to prevent it.

"Keep your eyes skinned," Davy advised. "The Atsinas might come back at any moment."

"Why would they?" Rebecca asked. "They've killed all my rescuers."

Had they, indeed? Davy had his doubts. Kayne, Norval, and Cyrus were missing. Striding to the west slope, he sought their bodies below, in vain. So there was a slim chance the trio had gotten away.

Flavius verified that an Atsina was dead by poking the warrior with his rifle. As he moved toward another, a glint of metal in the high grass lured him to a prize the Atsinas had overlooked in their haste to reclaim their female captive. "Look at this, pard!" he said, hoisting a long rifle chest high. "A present for you."

Davy accepted the gun gladly. Being unarmed in the wilds was akin to being naked. He helped himself to Craig's bullet pouch and powder horn. Added proof, if any were needed, that the Atsinas most definitely would return. The war party had neglected to strip the fallen of all their arms and other valuables.

"I count four dead Indians," Flavius announced.

That matched Davy's initial tally. The settlers had fared even worse, losing six men. "Hunt for a rifle for

Miss Worthington. And anything else that could come in handy."

Flavius remembered that Hillman had worn a new Green River knife in a shiny new sheath. But when he reached the body, knife and sheath were gone. So was a gold locket the man had worn containing a photograph of his wife.

A few yards to the south, Rebecca halted after making a wide circle of the battleground. "I don't see him here, do you?"

Davy was bent over another settler whose possibles bag had not been taken. Tugging on the strap, he idly glanced at her. "Which one?" he asked, figuring she was not aware that three settlers were missing.

"Pashipaho. The Sauk who abducted me."

"I haven't seen him since the shooting commenced," Davy said. "Why? Did you want to see his body for yourself?" Some women—and men—were like that. They were not satisfied until those who abused them were dead and gone.

Rebecca blinked in surprise. "His body? Gracious, no. I'm glad he escaped. He never did me any harm."

Why did Davy feel she was holding something back? He removed the possibles bag, slipped the strap over his arm, and adjusted it across his chest. "It's commendable you don't hold a grudge," he said. She began to answer, but a gasp choked it off.

From the vicinity of the gully wafted voices. The Atsina war party was returning.

Chapter Eight

Davy Crockett did not waste a second. Springing to Rebecca's side, he grabbed her wrist and pulled her toward the west slope. They went over the side without slowing.

Flavius did not need to be told to follow suit. Backpedaling to cover them, he spied vague movement off through the trees. Another few moments and the Atsinas would spot him. Flattening on his side, he rolled backward a good ten feet. He did not intend to roll past the crest, but gravity claimed him. Like an out-of-control barrel, he shot down the slope, gaining speed swiftly.

Davy and Rebecca were scrambling downward on the fly. A low squawk from Flavius alerted Davy to the two-legged avalanche about to slam into them. Throwing an arm around her, he jumped out of the way.

His momentum building, Flavius tried to arrest his

descent by gouging his elbows into the ground. All that did was spike pain clear up to his shoulders. In desperation, he jammed his rifle stock into the grass.

It worked. Sort of. The stock wedged against a bush or a mound or something. Flavius was not quite sure. But suddenly he was levered into the air, the rifle acting as a fulcrum. He managed to hold on to it as he tumbled end over end and crashed to a bruising stop against a small pine that cracked under the impact.

Dazed and hurting, Flavius sat up. His main worry was for his rifle and a pistol he had taken from a dead settler. As he examined them, Davy and the woman reached him.

"Did you bust anything?"

"I don't think so. My brainpan was rattled, but I'll live," Flavius said.

Rebecca glanced at the top of the hill. "Listen!" she whispered. "They must be close by."

The guttural tones of the Atsinas rang out crystal clear. Davy hauled Flavius to his feet and shoved him toward a row of trees fifteen feet below. "Hurry!" he urged.

Not that any urging was needed. Flavius and Rebecca were right on his heels as Davy rushed between a pair of closely spaced saplings and dropped onto his stomach. No sooner had they imitated him than several swarthy figures were silhouetted on the crest. One was much bigger than the others.

He-Bear, Davy guessed. The Big Belly leader took a few more steps, and Davy could see him clearly. He-Bear was scanning the slope. The big Atsina scowled, and when one of the warriors made a comment, He-Bear's reply was curt and harsh.

At a gesture from their chief, two Atsinas started down.

Rebecca grasped Davy's arm. "They've seen us!"

"No," Davy whispered. "They're just checking. Maybe they heard something when Flavius hit that tree."

"I didn't mean to," Flavius apologized, and grumbled, "Stupid place to put a tree, anyhow."

Davy set to loading his rifle. He had to be careful not to give himself away. The warriors were roving south of the tracks they had made, and had not yet seen the broken pine. As he capped the powder horn after pouring the proper amount down the barrel, he saw the leanest of the two meander northward.

"If he sees our scuff marks, it's root hog or die," Flavius whispered. He fixed a bead on the skinny one, his thumb curled around the hammer.

"Don't shoot unless I say to," Davy directed, busy with a patch and ball.

Rebecca was gnawing on her white knuckles. "Please, no!" she said quietly. "No more killing on my account!"

"I'll bet you can't wait to get home to Peoria," Davy remarked softly, and was puzzled when she started as if pricked with a pin and her eyes grew wide with consternation. What was that all about?

Davy forgot about her when the lean Atsina abruptly squatted and ran a hand over a patch of grass. At a word from him, the second warrior hastened to the spot. They consulted, and the lean one let out with a yell that brought He-Bear and the rest of the war party to the top of the slope.

"We're in for it now," Flavius breathed.

So it seemed. He-Bear limped down to the pair and inspected whatever they had found. Straightening, He-Bear surveyed the lower portion of the hill, his eyes roving over the saplings and on to dense vegetation to the south.

Flavius held his breath. Six against two were awful odds. Davy and he would drop two before the war party reached them, then it would be close-in fighting, knife and tomahawk work, and the Devil take the slowest.

Davy finished loading. Aligning the rifle, he centered the sights on He-Bear's broad chest just as the Atsina moved toward the saplings. *This is it*, Davy thought.

Then, to the south, a rifle shot echoed. The warriors all turned to scour the woodland below. They talked excitedly, growing more animated when the duller retort of a pistol rolled across the valley.

He-Bear glanced down the slope, then out over the woods. Davy touched his finger to the trigger, ready to put a ball between the Atsina's eyes if he made the wrong decision.

"Look! They're leaving!" Rebecca whispered.

That they were. The war party loped southward, He-Bear at the rear, his stiff leg slowing him so that he was the last to disappear into the verdant vegetation.

"We're safe!" Flavius gushed, letting out his breath in a whoosh. He was so happy, he forgot himself and clapped Rebecca on the back.

"Not yet we aren't," Davy said. Nor would they be until they reached the settlement.

"What were those shots?" Rebecca inquired.

Davy wished he knew. "No telling. Norval, Cyrus, and Kayne are out there somewhere. And a larger rescue party is supposedly on its way. Or maybe more Indians are in the area."

"More Sauks, most likely," Flavius said. "It's a shame we don't have wings on our feet like that Hermes feller our teacher told us about."

"Better yet, we could use a winged horse like that Pegasus," Davy joked.

Flavius sat up. He wanted to kick himself for plumb forgetting an important tidbit of information. "Our horses!" he blurted.

"What about them?"

"The Atsinas left them tied to a tree about half a mile north of the hill!" Flavius recollected. "If we can get to them first, those buzzards will eat our dust."

"Let's go." Davy boosted Rebecca to her feet. Her lips were compressed tightly, as they would be when someone was extremely upset and attempting not to show it. "Anything wrong?" he quizzed.

"No. I'm worn out, is all."

Flavius was his jovial self now that their escape was assured. "That makes two of us, ma'am," he said. "I'm so hungry, I could eat an elk whole, antlers and hooves and all."

"Since you know where the horses are, you guide us," Davy suggested, and fell into place behind Rebecca. Unaccountably, she dragged her heels, often hanging back when Flavius tried to set a brisk pace. It slowed them terribly. A trek that should have taken less than ten minutes took twice that long.

As near as Flavius could recall, the horses were in a glade fringed by a blackberry patch on the east and a mammoth maple on the west. He had not bothered to memorize any other landmarks, since at the time he had been bound and gagged and was constantly being prodded by a lance held by a warrior who took perverse pleasure in tormenting him.

So it took a while for Flavius to get his bearings. When the emerald crown of a maple hove into sight to the left, he slanted toward it. Maples that size were few and far between. It might be the right one.

Flavius was so eager to reach the horses and get

out of there that he barged through any brush and weeds in his path, making more noise than he normally would.

"Quiet down," Davy scolded at one point, but it was like talking to a brick. His friend plowed blithely on. Davy contented himself with keeping one eye on their back trail and the other on Rebecca Worthington.

The blonde acted more depressed the farther they went. Repeatedly she cast longing looks into the trees, as if in hope of seeing something—or someone.

Davy was at a loss to explain her behavior. Common politeness prevented him from prying, but when, for the tenth time, she gazed fervently into the trees and pouted, he could not contain himself. "What's eating at you, ma'am, if you don't mind my asking?"

Rebecca gazed straight ahead. "Nothing," she said stiffly.

Davy figured that was that, but in half a minute she cleared her throat and asked a question that no one had ever posed before.

"Are you happy with your life, Mr. Crockett?"

"Tolerably so, I reckon," Davy confessed. "I have a wife who darns my socks regularly, a passel of sprouts that keep my head spinning, and a comfortable cabin to live in. What more can a fellow ask for?"

"That's your definition of happiness, then? A family and a home?"

"Something wrong with that?"

Rebecca's long dress snagged on a bush, and she had to tug it loose. "No. Not at all. You've found your niche in life and you're content. I envy you. Not many can make the same claim."

Since she had broached the subject, Davy felt at liberty to ask, "How about you? Are you happy with your life?"

She bowed her head. Her hair covered most of her face, hiding her features when she said in the voice of a girl of ten or twelve, "I wish."

"Ma'am?"

"Living our lives as we see fit is a luxury most of us are denied, Mr. Crockett. Circumstances dictate what we do, not personal choice."

Davy disagreed. "A body can do whatever they want if they set their mind to it. Your life is your own. You can't live it the way others say you should or you'll always be miserable."

"How true," Rebecca said rather sadly. "But it's different for you, Mr. Crockett. Being a man, and all."

"You've lost me again."

Rebecca glanced back at him. "The rules are different for women. We're supposed to keep our place, to be obedient daughters, to always do whatever our parents want. We're not given the same freedom men are. And that's not fair."

"Comes a time when every person is old enough to move out on their own. Then you can do what *you* want."

A bitter laugh rippled from her velvet throat. "Oh, if only that were an option! But my parents, Mr. Crockett, see things differently. Before the year is out, they want me married off to a man I can't abide."

"Put your foot down," Davy said. It was a lame suggestion, but what else could she do? Other than leave home without her parents' blessing, and try to make do in a world that gulped innocent young women into its merciless maw and spit them out battered and broken?

Rebecca laughed louder. "Really, Mr. Crockett. If

you knew my father, you would appreciate how ridiculous that idea is. Festus Aloysius Worthington does not take guff from his offspring. Ever." She rubbed her left cheek. "The last time I had the gumption to sass him, he slapped me so hard I nearly lost a couple of teeth."

"I'm sorry for you," Davy said, and meant it. He never had cottoned to women-beaters.

"Not half as sorry as I am," Rebecca said.

Davy sought to cheer her by saying, "Don't give up. So long as you're breathing, there's hope." He saw Flavius slow down. "If a person wants something badly enough, they usually can get it. There's no bucking someone who knows their own mind and won't be stopped come hell or high water."

A pensive look came over her. "No, I guess there isn't. All we have to do is be willing to face the consequences."

Flavius halted and chuckled. Ahead was the glade, shaded by the high maple. On the other side were the sorrel and the bay, calmly grazing. "I did it!" he exclaimed, tickled with himself.

Davy moved past him, scouring the clearing. He was not taking any chances. Both horses raised their heads and stared at him, their ears pricked. "It's safe," he judged.

"You can ride my horse, miss," Flavius told Rebecca, since only the bay had a saddle.

"I don't mind riding double," Rebecca said.

A vivid image of trotting along with her glued to his back made Flavius break out in a cold sweat. Matilda would throw a fit if she heard.

Davy walked to the sorrel and reached out to unfasten the buckskin cord the Atsinas had used to tether the mounts. A loud metallic click from the blackberry bushes to his right riveted him where he stood.

"No one move!"

Flavius rotated, bringing up his rifle. Seeing the dark hole of a muzzle fixed on him was enough to convince him to comply. He froze.

Rebecca, however, did not. Squealing for joy, she dashed to the thicket. "Is it really you?" she asked, clapping her hands.

From out of the growth strode Pashipaho. The stately Sauk held a rifle at chest height. "I knew that whoever won would come for the horses, and bring you. So I waited."

Davy was astounded when the blonde threw herself at the warrior and lavished his cheek and neck with passionate kisses. "I must have missed something somewhere," he declared.

Pashipaho wagged the rifle. "Put your weapons on the ground. I have no desire to harm you, so do not do anything stupid."

One by one, Davy set his collection down. Flavius hastily did the same.

The Sauk visibly relaxed. Circling to the sorrel, he motioned for them to back up. "We meet again," he said to Flavius, grinning. "I am glad to see you alive."

"As if you care!" Flavius responded. "You were all fired up to turn me over to the Atsinas to be tortured, remember?"

Rebecca was leaning against the warrior, running her fingers along his turban. "He only did what he had to do to save me. Please don't hold it against him."

Insight filled Davy like water filling a pitcher. Hadn't John Kayne mentioned that Rebecca secretly cared for someone, and had for a long time? And that no one else in the settlement knew who the lucky man was? "The two of you have been in love for quite a spell, I hear."

The blonde and the warrior exchanged glances. "Who could have told you?" Rebecca asked. "We've kept it a secret from everyone, even our friends. We had to, or we both would have suffered."

"We must not hide it any longer," Pashipaho said. "We should live our lives as we want. We will go off by ourselves and find a place where we can live in peace."

Rebecca stepped away from him, amazement and affection radiating from her like sunshine from the sun. "Do you mean it, Pashipaho?"

"I do."

"It's a dream come true!" Rebecca cried, and embraced him, inadvertently pinning his arms to his sides in the process.

Davy glanced down. This was the opening he needed. He could pick up the rifle and snap off a shot before the warrior did, but he did not try. The Sauk had promised not to harm them, and he took the man at his word.

Rebecca, giggling in childlike glee, turned, her hand gripping the warrior's. "I want you to understand, Mr. Crockett. Pashipaho and I met years ago, shortly after my pa moved us here from Ohio. I'm not a big believer in Cupid or any of that stuff, but I fell in love with him the second I saw him."

"And I with her," Pashipaho said in his cultured English.

"For a long time nothing came of it," Rebecca continued. "We'd look at each other, and we could tell how we felt, but we dared not let on. My pa would have broken both my legs if he found out. And Pashipaho's people don't much like whites."

"There is too much hatred on both sides," the warrior remarked.

Rebecca was positively bubbling with the need to share her tale. "Two summers ago, the settlement held a social. The parson invited a few friendly Indians. Among them were Pashipaho's pa and ma." Her voice acquired a dreamy aspect. "We avoided each other most of the dance. Then, somehow, we bumped into each other outside. Before I knew what was happening, I was in his arms."

"I was to blame," the Sauk said. "She was so beautiful, with the moonlight on her hair and her face shining like the moon itself."

If ever Davy had met two people in love, these two qualified.

"We snuck out to meet from time to time," Rebecca said. "We always figured that we would work it out, that we would be husband and wife one day." The light faded from her face. "Up until the morning my pa announced that I was to marry Cyrus Binderhorn, whether I liked the idea or not."

It was Pashipaho's turn to become grave. "When I heard, my mind was in a whirl. I could not eat. I could not sleep. I did not know what to do."

"So you decided to steal her so she wouldn't have to wed Cyrus," Davy speculated.

The Sauk nodded. "It seemed like the right thing to do at the time."

Flavius had been listening with half an ear. Talk of romance invariably bored him, and now that he was not in immediate danger, his thoughts had strayed to food. "What did I tell you?" he said to Davy. "Doing right ain't always bright."

"And doing wrong is?" Davy challenged. To the lovebirds he had more to say. "All this is well and good, but you've brought grief down on a lot of innocent people. Think of those dead men up on the hill. What about their families? What about the kin of the Atsinas who were killed?"

"It couldn't be helped," Rebecca said. "Things got of out hand, is all. If I could turn back time, I would. But I can't, so now we have to make the best of it."

"I tried to avoid spilling blood," Pashipaho remarked. "I did not want to give her people more reason to hate me." He sighed forlornly. "Bad medicine has ruined everything."

Davy understood now why the Sauk had not harmed Rebecca's father. And why Pashipaho had not allowed the other Sauks to take his life, or to slay Flavius. "What do you plan to do?"

"We will go far, far away," the warrior stated. "Somewhere the people do not know us. Somewhere we can live together in peace."

Flavius had heard some harebrained notions in his time, but theirs beat all. "Lord love a duck!" he declared. "What planet do you two think you're living on, anyhow? Once word gets out how you misled everybody, the folks hereabouts will be mad enough to eat nails and spit tacks. They won't rest until they hunt you down."

Pashipaho grew troubled. His brows knit, and he looked long and hard at the rifle he held, a rifle Davy recognized as belonging to one of the slain settlers.

"Making yourselves scarce is best for everyone," Davy said, his intuition blaring like the foghorn on a ship.

"We'll need your horses, though," Rebecca said, moving to the bay. "Hope you don't mind."

Panic welled up in Flavius. Without mounts it would take them a year of Sundays to reach Tennessee, and they did not have enough money between them to buy a single new animal. "Now, hold on there," he protested. "We need those critters. Go steal someone else's."

"Be reasonable. Where would we go to find them? Back at the settlement? At Pashipaho's village?" Rebecca grasped the reins and grabbed hold of the saddle to pull herself up. "I'm truly sorry."

"Not sorry enough," Flavius groused as she climbed on. There went his saddle and what few personal effects he had.

Rebecca rode around the Sauk, who had not budged, then drew rein. "What's wrong? Why are you just standing there? Mount up. The Atsinas will be coming to claim these animals before too long."

Pashipaho widened his stance, his dark eyes narrowing. "We should not leave witnesses."

"What?" Rebecca twisted. "You can't."

"Think, dear one. Only these two know we are still alive. Only these two know we have taken the horses. If we shoot them, your people will blame the Atsinas. We will be free."

Davy tucked his knees a few inches, tensing to scoop up his rifle. Plainly, he had grossly misjudged the Sauk.

"No!" Rebecca said. "You haven't killed anyone yet. Why start now?" Her voice quaked with anxiety. When the warrior did not answer, she said, "If you shoot them, Pashipaho, you're not the man I believe you are, and I want nothing more to do with you."

The Sauk frowned. Reluctantly, he slowly lowered the rifle. Lithely swinging onto the sorrel, he trotted to the northeast, the woman who had forsaken her own kind for the sake of his love at his side.

Davy watched until they were out of sight. He did not attempt to grab a weapon, not with Pashipaho glancing back every few yards. When the horses were shrouded by growth, he summed up his feelings by flinging his arms heavenward and bellowing, "Damn!"

"What now, partner?" Flavius asked.

"What else?" Davy kicked the ground in anger. "They left us no choice. Without those horses, we might as well stay in Illinois. We're going after them."

"And if the lady and her man friend raise a fuss?"

"We take what's ours. One way or the other."

Chapter Nine

It seemed like a scatterbrained notion. Two men on foot, no matter how fast they were, could never hope to overtake a pair of horses.

But the woodland in that locale was particularly thick. The dense undergrowth and tightly spaced trees would slow the sorrel and the bay, would force Pashipaho and Rebecca Worthington to hold the animals to a brisk walk, at best.

Davy retrieved everything he had been forced to drop and lit out, plunging into the forest at the exact point they had.

"Hold on!" Flavius hollered, bending to grab his rifle. He did not care to be left behind, not with the Atsina war party still on the loose and thirsting for white blood. Hastily following, he frowned when his friend melted into the greenery. He knew that he must follow as best he could. The Irishman wasn't about to slow down on his account.

Blood Hunt

A carpet of pine needles and fallen leaves enabled Davy to move silently. He traveled over a hundred yards, then glimpsed movement. The fleeing pair were riding as rapidly as the terrain allowed. Rebecca was lighthearted, feeling they were safe; she chattered like a chipmunk. Pashipaho, however, was wiser. The warrior rode alertly, repeatedly glancing over his shoulder.

Davy stayed low, using the cover to its best advantage, flattening whenever the Sauk started to turn. It would have been child's play to put a ball into Pashipaho's back, but he didn't. Killing someone from ambush simply wasn't in his nature.

Eventually the pair would stop, and that was when Davy would make his move. He figured they would keep going for quite some time and had just resigned himself to hours of tiring pursuit, when to his surprise the sorrel nickered loudly and Pashipaho promptly reined up.

Rebecca cried out, words Davy did not quite catch. She vaulted from the bay and dashed forward to kneel beside a small log.

The saints be praised! Davy thought. He had them! Gliding noiselessly to the left, within moments he was close enough to see that the object he had mistaken for a log was actually a man, lying on his side. Davy stalked closer, halting behind an oak.

Rebecca was staring in disbelief at Pashipaho. "You can't be serious!" she said. "We've got to do something. If we don't, he'll die."

The Sauk's features grew hard. "I am sorry. We must get away while we can. You are more important to me than anyone else."

"But he's my uncle," Rebecca said, and rolled the limp form over.

Norval Worthington was unconscious, a nasty

gash on his forehead caked with dry blood. A knife wound high in his chest had stained half his shirt.

Rebecca bent over her kin. "He's hurt bad, but with our help he can pull through. I won't let him die, Pashipaho. Norval has always been kind to me. Twice he stopped my pa from taking a switch to my back. I love him."

The Sauk stiffly dismounted. "Your soft heart will be the death of us." Handing her his rifle, he hunkered and slipped his arms under the settler. "There is a stream to the northeast. We will take him there to clean his wounds."

Davy picked that moment to stride into the open and level his gun. "You're going to have some company, whether you want some or not."

Both spun. Rebecca began to bring up the rifle but thought better of the idea. Pashipaho grabbed for the knife on his hip, stopping when Davy shook his head.

"I'd rather not shoot you unless you're real partial to taking some lead. All we want is what's rightfully ours."

"Without your horses, the Atsinas will catch us," Pashipaho said angrily.

"Not if you're a smidgen as clever as I think you are," Davy responded. "You know this area like the back of your hand. The Atsinas don't. Losing them should be as easy as licking butter off a knife."

The crash of brush announced the arrival of Flavius. He had heard voices and put on a burst of speed. Puffing like a fish out of water, he trained his rifle on the turbaned Sauk. "I heard what you said. So pull that pigsticker, if you want. I'm not as forgiving as my pard. I'd as soon snuff your wick for what you've done."

Rebecca was more practical than the man who had claimed her heart. "We can make do without the horses," she told him. "Please, for my sake, let it be."

Pashipaho released the knife, but sparks flickered in the depths of his dark eyes.

"Shed it, and the rest of your weapons," Davy directed. "We'll give them back when we go our separate ways. Not before."

"Turnabout is fair play, I suppose," Rebecca said, grinning. She had to nudge Pashipaho before he would draw his knife and cast it down.

"Take us to the stream," Davy said. "Once we revive Norval, we'll get him to Peoria."

While Flavius covered the Sauk, Davy and Rebecca boosted Norval onto the sorrel, draping him over the saddle. Davy asked her to lead the horse, which she gladly did.

Flavius was overjoyed to be astride the bay. He'd rather ride than walk any day. Rifle cocked and ready, he didn't take his eyes off the Sauk once.

Forty-five minutes later, the woodland thinned near the low bank of a bubbling blue ribbon that bordered a narrow lush meadow rife with wildflowers and butterflies.

Davy made Pashipaho sit on a stump near the water. Lowering Norval, he peeled off the man's shirt. The knife had bit deep but had spared major arteries and organs. The head wound worried him more. Although the gash was not severe, sometimes blows to the head resulted in brain damage. He recollected an acquaintance who had received a glancing tomahawk blow to the noggin during the Creek War. The man had not been gravely hurt. Yet when the fellow revived, his mind was gone. The woodsman had been left a human vegetable.

Rebecca brought wood for the fire. Flavius lent her the tinder box, fire steel, and a flint from the possibles bag he carried.

Frontier women were versed in a variety of tasks. Learning to start fires was paramount, for without fire, meals couldn't be cooked, clothes couldn't be properly washed, and no one could indulge in the luxury of a hot bath.

At an early age girls were taught how to apply kindling, how to strike a slicing blow with the steel against the flint, how to fan sparks with light puffs of breath so the kindling would flare and set the wood ablaze.

Soon a small fire crackled warmly. After filling Flavius's coffeepot with water, Rebecca heated it. From the hem of her dress she cut a three-inch strip over a foot long. This she wet and used to clean her uncle's wounds.

Norval groaned when she pressed the folded cloth to his head. He mumbled and shifted but did not come around.

All this while, Pashipaho sat and glared, a wolf at bay. Flavius made it a point to always keep the Sauk in sight. The warrior was just itching for a chance to jump them, and Flavius was not going to give it to him.

A stand of cottonwoods flanked the stream. Davy selected the highest and shimmied up it, just as he had done countless times as a boy when frolicking in the woods around the family cabin.

Near the top the slim bole curled under his weight, so he stopped and gazed out over a billowy sea of green canopies, broken here and there by clearings. A hump on the horizon marked the location of the hill. Other than birds and squirrels and deer, no living creatures were abroad.

Davy stayed in his roost for close to five minutes. When he was fairly confident the war party was not in their immediate vicinity, he climbed down.

Rebecca had made a pillow of her uncle's shirt and slid it under his head. She was wringing her make-shift towel, and looked up at Davy's approach. Nodding at Pashipaho, she commented, "You must despise us like sin for what we've done, Mr. Crockett."

"Hate is an expensive proposition, ma'am. It's sort of like setting your innards on fire. It burns a body all up inside, and never does much more than make you miserable."

"Was your father a preacher?"

Davy chuckled. "Goodness, no. He was a ranger during the revolution against the British. After that he tried his hand at various ways of being poor."

It was Rebecca's turn to chuckle. Then she said, "Has anyone ever mentioned that you have a colorful way with words? Maybe you should be a writer."

The suggestion caused Davy to slap his leg and laugh. "I'd be the worst who ever took up a quill pen. My problem is that I'd never spell a word the same way twice."

"You haven't had much schooling, I take it?"

"No more than was forced on me," Davy admitted. "I turned sour on schooling right early. Blame me, since to hear the schoolmaster tell it, he was the greatest orator to come along since man grew a tongue."

Norvall Worthington stirred, ending their conversation. Opening his eyes, he regarded them a bit. "So I'm not in the hereafter?" he said with a wry smirk. "I reckoned I was a goner, for sure."

"How did you get away?" Davy asked.

Norvall's brow creased. "I don't rightly know. I remember He-Bear stabbed me. I fell, and crawled past the fire." Weakly, he lifted a hand to his forehead to touch the damp strip. "Something brushed my legs.

I glanced up, and saw one of those red devils holding a war club. After that, everything is all jumbled."

"He must have hit you and knocked you down the hill," Davy guessed.

"Probably. I seem to recall getting up and running until I couldn't run any longer." Grimacing, Norval twisted his head and saw Flavius holding a rifle on Pashipaho. "Where is everybody else? What happened?"

Briefly, Davy related the disaster, concluding with "Cyrus, Kayne, and you were the only ones unaccounted for. I was hoping the three of you were together."

Norval attempted to sit up. Grunting, he rose partway, then collapsed, gritting his teeth. "Damn! I'm so dizzy, I can't hardly think."

"Take it easy, Uncle," Rebecca said. "There's no rush. As soon as you're up to it, these gentlemen from Tennessee are going to see you safely to the settlement."

"And what about you, Niece?" Norval asked. "Are you going back to your pa? Or are you traipsing off with that mangy Sauk?"

Rebecca tensed. "You know?"

"Hell, girl. A blind man would have noticed how the two of you were always making cow eyes at one another." Norval licked his dry lips. "Let's just say I suspected all along. And when your pa described who jumped him, it didn't take a Ben Franklin to figure out what was what."

"But you never let on?"

"Why should I? You're a grown woman. It's high time you stand on your own two feet and do as you want, not as your pa dictates." Norval gave the warrior a withering glare. "But I can't say much of the choice you've made."

"I love him, Uncle."

"So? What does love have to do with anything? You're letting yourself in for a life of pure hell. Find one of your own kind, someone who has decent table manners and won't work you to death. In a few years you'll care for him just as much as you do this heathen."

"Never."

Norval motioned sharply. "Trust me, girl. I'm a lot older than you. I've seen it happen more times than I could count. Many a marriage has started out with the husband and wife hardly liking each other. But in time love sprouts, just like a seed. Plant it in your heart and it will take root."

"I care for Pashipaho," Rebecca insisted.

Exasperated, Norval looked at Davy. "Tell her, Crockett. She'll be shunned by her own people. Whites don't want anything to do with women who take up with Indians of their own free will. They'll brand her a harlot, or worse."

"Do you think I don't know that?" Rebecca said. "I'm willing to bear the consequences."

"So you think," Norval argued. "But you have no idea what you're letting yourself in for. It will be worse than anything you can imagine. The day will come when you'll rue the choice you've made."

"Maybe so. But until that day, I'm staying with Pashipaho."

Norval faced the Sauk. "What about you, Indian? Do you care for my niece?"

The warrior was as self-assured as the woman he adored. "She is the sun and the moon, the rainbow and the dawn. Do not fear. She will always have a lodge roof over her head, and her belly will never be empty. This I pledge."

"Idiots!" Norval muttered. "You're a pair of young

idiots." He shook a fist at Pashipaho. "What about your own kind? What about those who will look down their noses at her because she's white? What about those who will want her *dead*? Will you be with her every minute of every day to protect her?"

The Sauk's jaw jutted out. "We do not intend to live among my people. We are going off by ourselves."

"Wonderful!" Norval said bitterly. "And who will be there to lend a hand when you need it? Who will act as midwife when Rebecca gives birth? Who will your kids play with as they grow up? Who will you rely on when disease strikes? Or calamity befalls you?"

"We will depend on each other," Pashipaho said.

Shaking his head, Norval sank back. "Children! I'm dealing with children here!" Grasping Rebecca's hand, he tenderly stroked it. "Listen to me, girl. Please. Love isn't enough. It doesn't mean you'll live a charmed life. It won't put food on your table. It won't spare you or your children from being massacred—"

Norval would have rambled on, but Rebecca rested a finger across his lips. "Enough, Uncle. You need to rest. We'll talk more later."

"Damned right we will," Norval said, and drifted off as soon as he closed his eyes. Rebecca folded his hands on his stomach and kissed his forehead.

Davy sensed that both she and the Sauk were bothered by the old man's plea, but neither brought it up. The warrior turned his back to them, his shoulders slumped. Rebecca, rising, stepped toward her man, then abruptly changed direction. She strolled to the stream instead, and stood peering intently into a small pool, as if seeking answers in its depths.

Flavius agreed with the grizzled settler one hundred percent. It would be a cold day in Hades before he'd agree to any daughter of his wedding an Indian. The blonde and the Sauk were too naive to see that Norval had only their best interests at heart.

The horses had drifted westward. Davy went to fetch them, ambling along the bank to where part of it had collapsed, forming an earthen ramp.

Davy happened to look down, and halted. Newly imprinted in the damp soil at the stream's edge was a single track, made by a man wearing moccasins. He recognized the outline of a Sauk moccasin, with its distinctive curved toe.

Davy pivoted. Pashipaho had not budged since sitting on the stump. Which meant another Sauk had made the print. Scouring the bank, Davy found more a little farther on. A sizable band had crossed the stream at that point, less than an hour ago, heading eastward.

Whether it was a hunting party or a war party was irrelevant. Especially if the Sauks had heard the distant gunfire. They would prowl the woods until they located whoever was responsible.

As if Davy did not have enough to worry about! Hastening to the horses, he led them back and tied them securely to a low limb. Rebecca and Pashipaho were shoulder to shoulder, speaking in hushed tones.

Flavius had moved to the fire but had not taken his eyes off the pair. He straightened in bewilderment when Davy suddenly upended the coffeepot over the flames, smothering them. "What the blazes?" he blurted.

"Sauks in the area," Davy explained, kicking the drenched brands to scatter them and minimize the smoke.

"Damn!" Flavius groused. "When it rains, it pours."

He jabbed a thumb at the warrior and the woman. "Are we really just going to let them waltz on off?"

"What else would you have us do?" Davy asked.

The whispered response came not from Flavius, but from the battered man at their feet. "Kill Pashi-paho."

Davy knelt beside Norval. "In cold blood?"

"It's for her own good," the settler quietly urged. "She's too immature to know what's best. If she runs off with that red buzzard, she's doomed to a life of woe."

"I won't play God."

"Who's asking you to?" Norval said. His imploring gaze drifted from one Tennessean to the other. "Hell, if you boys ain't got the stomach for it, then lend me a gun. I'll do the job myself, here and now."

"She'd never forgive you," Davy remarked.

"That's my cross to bear. At least when I pass on, I'll go to meet my Maker knowing that I gave her the gift of a life worth living."

Flavius was torn by the oldster's appeal. It might be doing the woman a favor, true enough. But Davy had a point, too. Who were they to usurp the role of the Almighty?

"Please," Norval implored. "A pistol will do. You can turn your backs until it's over so no one can hold you to blame."

"Except our own consciences," Davy said. "No, it's wrong. Their fate is in the hands of Providence. We'll not lift a finger against them."

Norval wrung his hands and sank onto his back. "If that was your daughter or niece, you'd do it. You're weak, Crockett. You've no gumption."

Davy was unfazed by the insult. "Maybe so, but I'll sleep better at night." He looked toward the stump, thinking he should allow the lovers to leave before

Norval found a means to do something they would all regret, and was nonplussed to see them fording the stream.

"Wait!" Davy cried, springing erect.

Heedless of the command, Pashipaho and Rebecca bolted, quickly gaining the forest. The Sauk shot a grin of triumph at the white men.

"No!" Davy shouted, giving chase. The fools were leaving unarmed. And they were heading eastward, in the same direction taken by the Sauk band. "Not that way!"

Splashing across, Davy reached the trees seconds after they did. Yet they were not in sight. He crashed into the brush, following their sign. The tracks and crushed grass lasted for nine or ten feet, then nothing. The trail ended in thin air.

It couldn't be! Davy mused. Stooping, he inspected the last few footprints and discovered a double heel print on those left by Rebecca.

They had walked backward in their own tracks, Pashipaho so perfectly that his double prints were as one. Rebecca did not have as much practice; she gave it away. Davy backtracked a couple of yards to where they had jumped onto a long log that lay at right angles to their original bearing. They had scooted along the log and in among pines.

The short delay proved costly. Davy pushed himself but could not overtake them, and in due course he broke into the open to learn that he had been royally duped.

All this time the stream had been to his left. But here it bore eastward in a lopsided loop. Pashipaho had led Rebecca into the middle, where the swiftly flowing water had erased every last trace of their passage.

Figuring they had gone eastward, Davy did likewise. Within sixty feet, though, he gave up. There was no predicting where the pair would climb out. He'd need to scour both banks for miles, and even then he had no guarantee of picking up their trail again.

Profoundly disappointed, Davy trudged back to camp. Flavius anxiously awaited him, fingering the rifle. Norval had sat up and was chewing on his lower lip. "Well?" both queried in unison.

Davy shook his head.

"Damn that Indian to hell!" fumed the uncle. "This is all your fault, Crockett! You wouldn't shoot him when I asked! Who knows what will happen to that poor girl?"

"She's a grown woman," Davy echoed Rebecca's own sentiments. "She can take care of herself."

"Hogwash! She wouldn't last a minute against hostiles. That is, if they didn't keep her alive for fouler purposes." Agitated, Norval struggled to stand, opening his chest wound, which bled freely. "I hold you to blame if anything happens to her!"

"Sit down," Davy said, pushing on the settler's shoulders. "She'll be fine."

As if on cue, to the east rose a series of bloodcurdling yips and yells. On their heels rang a piercing scream, the heart-wrenching shriek of a woman in mortal terror.

Chapter Ten

Davy Crockett snaked past a tree, through a patch of tall weeds, then to the bottom of a low mound choked with clover and flowers. Crawling to the top, Davy carefully parted some of the stems and peered at the scene in the meadow beyond.

Seven Sauks were gathered around a shapely blond figure lying on her side. Rebecca Worthington's hair was in disarray, her clothes askew. She had a bruise on her cheek, and was fearfully regarding the ring of burnished warriors.

Next to her, on his knees, was Pashipaho. He, too, had been roughed up, and over him stood a burly, sneering Sauk who was going on at some length about something or other in their own tongue.

"What do they want, dearest?" Rebecca asked Pashipaho. "What is he saying?"

The burly specimen hiked a hand as if to cuff her. She recoiled, and he smiled. "I will tell you, white bitch," he snarled in clipped, slurred English.

Pashipaho tensed to fling himself at her tormentor. "Do not touch her again, Niaga." In their own language he made a comment that caused the other warriors to swap uneasy looks.

Niaga shoved his face in front of Pashipaho's and taunted him, saying, "What if we do? What will you do? Would you lift a hand against your own brothers?"

"Do not make me choose between you," Pashipaho declared. "You know I love her."

Niaga straightened. "How can a Sauk love a *white*?" Giving no hint of what he was going to do, he suddenly turned and kicked Rebecca in the thigh. She clutched her leg and cried out. Instantly Pashipaho threw himself at her tormentor, but two warriors seized him by the arms before he could strike. He struggled to break their grip, and had nearly succeeded when a third man clamped him on the back of the neck. Pashipaho stopped resisting.

"Look at you!" Niaga said, jabbing a finger into Pashipaho's chest. "Ready to fight *us*, over *her*!" So incensed was he that he kicked Rebecca again. She had the presence of mind to curl into a ball, and did not lash out.

"Stop!" Pashipaho raged, once more striving to break loose.

Niaga, flushed with anger, was about to kick Rebecca a third time, but he lowered his foot. "She will never see her own kind again," he announced.

Rebecca glanced up. "Why? What have I ever done to you, Niaga?"

"Done?" the burly warrior repeated scornfully. "You do not need to *do* anything. It is enough that you have white skin."

"That's all you have against me?" Rebecca asked.

"You loathe me because I'm a white woman?"

"That is reason enough," Niaga said. "All my people hate your people. All, except for him." He gestured in contempt at Pashipaho. "Once, woman, he was my friend. Once, we roamed these hills day after day. Once, we hunted together, went on raids together. Once, we shared dreams. Then he met you, and you stole his mind."

Pashipaho came to her defense. "That is not true! If she stole anything, it was my heart."

Niaga did not seem to hear. Leaning over Rebecca, he said barely loud enough for Davy to hear, "Long have I hoped he would come to his senses. Long have I hoped he would take a Sauk woman into his lodge and forget he ever saw you."

"I have a right to love who I want! To live as I want!" Pashipaho said.

Niaga sobered and pursed his lips. "Not when in doing so you bring shame on our people. Not when you want to lie each night with a white dog at your side." He placed a hand on the taller warrior's shoulder. "Think, old friend. Think of the shame you bring to yourself, to your father, to our people. We could not bear to have her in our village. We could not bear to be reminded every day of all the whites have done to us."

"But we are not going to the village," Pashipaho said. "We are leaving this territory. We will go far away and start new lives."

Niaga apparently translated for the benefit of the Sauks who did not speak English. Their mutual disdain was apparent. "Has it come to this, then?" Niaga said. "You would desert your own for one of theirs? You would turn your back on your family, on your friends, and go off with one of our sworn enemies?"

Pashipaho reared defiantly. "I will not give her up," he stated.

"Is that so?"

"Let us go in peace, Niaga," Pashipaho entreated. "No harm will come of it. And you will never set eyes on us again."

"No harm?" the burly warrior said. "The memory of how you turned against your own will be with me to the end of my life." He motioned, and another warrior slid behind Rebecca and hauled her upright.

Alarmed, Pashipaho asked urgently, "What do you plan to do?"

"Save you from yourself." Niaga slowly drew a long, gleaming blade. "With this bitch dead, you will come to your senses."

"No!" Pashipaho pleaded.

"You will hate me for a while," Niaga said, "but later you will see that I was right. And you will thank me." Hefting the bone-handled knife, he stepped in front of Rebecca. "I will make this quick so there is little pain."

Pashipaho went berserk. Like a madman, he heaved and kicked and thrashed, spinning every which way, and nearly succeeded in tossing the three warriors from him. At that moment a fourth knelt and grabbed him around the shins. Helpless, eyes wide, he watched as Niaga teasingly waved the razor tip of the knife an inch from the woman he adored.

To her credit, Rebecca did not cringe. Body rigid, fists balled, she glared at the man about to torture her.

Davy Crockett dared wait no longer. Cocking the rifle, he rose and took a hasty bead on Niaga. The Sauks were so intent on their victim that none was aware of his presence until he hollered, "Is that any way to treat a lady?"

The warriors whirled and looked up, but taken aback, they were slow to react. Then two started toward him, halting at a word from Niaga, who had not missed the significance of the leveled muzzle.

"That's right," Davy said. "You'll be the first to die if they don't do exactly as I say."

"Who are you, white man?" Niaga demanded. "What do you want?"

Davy answered in a lusty roar. "I'm a ring-tailed coon from Tennessee. I'm half horse, half alligator. I wrestle snapping turtles for fun and ride lightning bolts when I can't find a turtle."

The ploy worked. Confusion slowed Niaga, who did not seem to know quite what to make of the boast. It bought Davy time to descend the mound.

"I'm bad medicine for anyone who mistreats a woman," Davy said. "So step back and lower that tickler, or I'll part your turban with lead."

Niaga surveyed the woodland surrounding them. "Can it be? You are alone?" he said incredulously. "Yet you think you will stop us?"

"I don't *think* I will," Davy said, lowering his cheek to the rifle and curling his finger around the trigger. "I *know* I will. Now, let her go and have your friends step back or there will be hell to pay."

Davy counted on Niaga not being particularly eager to die. Should the whole band rush him at once, he'd nail one or two, but the rest would swarm over him before he could blink.

Niaga knew that too. "Shoot me, white man, and you, too, will be slain," he said nonchalantly. "Lower your rifle. We will talk."

"Pshaw!" Davy bantered. "If I lower my gun, I'm a goner." He did tilt the barrel, though, just enough so that it was aimed at Niaga's crotch. "Ever hope to have kids?" he quipped.

Raw hatred contorted Niaga. Stepping to one side, he spoke in the Sauk language to the others. A few moved back, but the rest balked. Notable among them were two younger warriors who were just itching to attack. One fondled a lance, the other carried a war club.

"Warn them," Davy cautioned. "It's your life if they get their dander up."

Niaga spoke more severely. To a man, the warriors backed away, but only a few feet.

Pashipaho enfolded Rebecca in his arms. Shielding her, he retreated toward the mound. Afraid for her safety, he did not take his eyes off his fellow Sauks, and that proved to be a mistake. For as he backed off, he blundered between Davy and Niaga, blocking Davy's shot.

A war whoop tore from the burly warrior's throat. Immediately the six other Sauks charged, voicing war cries of their own.

Davy had to take a sideways step in order to fix a bead on the foremost man. The warrior swept a tomahawk on high. At the crack of the Kentucky, the Sauk crumpled and pitched forward, limbs twitching.

Another warrior closed on Rebecca. A glittering blade sought her body. It cleaved downward, only to be countered by Pashipaho, who grasped the man's arm. Locked together, they grappled.

"Run, woman, run!" Davy urged, dashing to her aid. Rebecca had tripped over her own feet and was down on a knee. She raised horrified eyes to a young warrior about to smite her with a war club.

Davy's first pistol flashed clear. It belched lead and smoke, skewering the warrior in the stomach. The man tottered, fingers covering a neat hole that oozed crimson.

Three Sauks skirted their stricken companion and converged on Davy. He had borrowed Flavius's pistol before he set out, and he now unlimbered it with uncanny speed. The fleetest warrior was almost on top of him when he fired, the heavy ball sheering into the man's ribs and spinning him like a child's top.

Davy's guns were empty, useless. Releasing the second pistol, he gripped the rifle barrel and wielded it like a club. His swing, powered by tempered sinews, caught a Sauk on the chin.

That left one, who was out for blood. Davy swung again, but the warrior ducked and speared a lance at his stomach. Backpedaling, Davy battered the lance aside, again and again. The snarling Sauk pressed him, forcing him backward.

Davy was vaguely aware that Pashipaho still grappled with a determined foe, and that the Sauk he had clipped on the chin was slowly rising.

He had to dispatch his adversary right away. But the lance afforded the warrior a greater reach, which the man capitalized on by staying well back and thrusting.

The rifle parried lunge after lunge. Davy twisted as the spear point streaked past his hip. He took another step and came to the mound. Cornered, he delivered a flurry of wide sweeps that held the lance at bay.

Frustrated, the Sauk danced to the right and speared his weapon in low and fast. Davy had to hop to avoid being skewered, and retaliated with a sweep that knocked the lance to the left.

For a twinkling the warrior was off guard, the lance unbalanced. Dropping the rifle, Davy sprang. His tomahawk molded to the palm of his hand like a glove. He tried to split the man's skull, but the Sauk evaded him and produced a tomahawk too.

Circling, they feinted and clashed, taking each other's measure. Neither presented an opening the other could exploit.

Fearful of taking a knife or lance, Davy feinted to the right, then *went* right. The gambit was not a complete success. He connected, but it was a shallow blow to the rib cage. The warrior hardly flinched.

A woman's scream galvanized Davy into adopting a desperate measure. He threw his tomahawk, as he had at knots on trees and other targets for hours on end. It spun like a pinwheel, the keen edge sinking into the Sauk below the collarbone.

Davy did not wait to see his enemy fall. Spinning, he saw Pashipaho battling furiously with the warrior he had clipped on the jaw. Pashipaho's original foe was prone, a scarlet pool spreading under the body. And forty feet off, Rebecca wrestled in Niaga's iron grip.

The burly Sauk had her by the wrist and was endeavoring to drag her into the forest. Davy flew toward them. Niaga, hissing like a serpent, shoved her to the ground and turned to confront him, drawing a knife.

Davy flourished his own. Darting in low and hard, he slashed at Niaga's midsection. The Sauk slipped aside, pivoted, and drove his knife downward. A stinging sensation in Davy's side warned him that the thrust had nearly been fatal. He sidestepped to gain distance between them and accidentally trod on Rebecca, who was rising. Her legs snagged his. They sprawled in a heap.

Davy heard Niaga's howl of victory and looked around just as Niaga was about to cut him. Salvation came courtesy of a tall figure who shot like a cannonball out of nowhere to slam into Niaga.

Pashipaho was fury incarnate. He seized Niaga's

wrist to prevent his former friend from employing the knife, then wrapped his other hand around Niaga's throat. In turn, Niaga locked his free hand on Pashipaho's neck.

Davy untangled himself and rose, pulling Rebecca along with him. She tried to go to Pashipaho, but Davy would not let her. The outcome was in her lover's hands. Literally.

Both Sauks strained and wheezed, the corded muscles in their arms bulging, as were the veins in their temples. They rolled back and forth, side to side. One second Pashipaho was on top, the next, Niaga.

"Help him!" Rebecca wailed.

"It's his to do," Davy said, and was kicked in the ankle. Forking an arm around her waist, he ducked his head to absorb a hailstorm of punches. Fortunately, her strength did not match her rage.

Pashipaho and Niaga continued to wage their private war. Both were beet red and finding it steadily more difficult to breathe. Niaga, sputtering noisily, rammed a knee into Pashipaho's back—several times. The latter seemed not to feel it.

Then, the culmination. Pashipaho bunched his shoulder in a supreme effort. His fingers sank so deep into Niaga's neck, they disappeared. Niaga erupted in a frenzy and let go of Pashipaho's neck to batter his head and face. But the blows were feeble and became more so.

Knowing what was to occur, Davy attempted to pull Rebecca away so she need not see. She resisted. Pashipaho's wrist gave a sharp twist and the fight was over. Niaga went limp, his eyes registering amazement.

Pashipaho slowly sat up. He pried his fingers from his friend, leaving gouge marks and discolored flesh.

Shock set in. Soft words spilled from him in his own tongue.

"Pashipaho!" Rebecca cried.

The warrior did not answer. Gently, he touched Niaga's cheek. In English, he said in a strained tone, "Niaga! What have I done!"

Rebecca dug her nails into Davy's arm, and he relented. She promptly dashed to her man and draped a slender arm over his broad shoulder. "What's wrong?" she said plaintively. "You did what you had to do. It was either him or you."

In a daze, Pashipaho stared at her. "Do you not understand?" he replied. "He was my friend. The *best* friend I ever had. Now I have killed him."

"But he would have slain you," Rebecca pointed out. Dismayed, she hugged her warrior, and was rudely startled when he shrugged from her grasp and pushed her away.

Touching a hand to his brow, Pashipaho rose unsteadily. "Has it come to this, then?" he asked himself aloud. "Is my happiness worth the lives of my brothers?"

"What are you saying?" Rebecca said, clutching his shirt. "Don't you want to go off with me? Have you given up on our dream?"

Pashipaho looked down at Niaga and groaned. Swaying like a forest giant about to topple, he reeled backward as if drunk and reached for support that was not there. "What will my father say? What will my sisters say?"

Tears trickled down Rebecca's cheeks. "Don't torment yourself so. We knew that something like this could happen at any time."

"Yes, but . . ." Pashipaho's voice trailed off as he staggered to the mound and sat facing the bodies. "I will be cast from my tribe. From this day on, I can never go back again."

Rebecca ran to him, knelt, and took his large hands in hers. "You have *me*," she declared, but it did not dispel his melancholy.

Davy reclaimed his guns and reloaded them. One of the Sauks commenced to moan, another to move weakly. Examining both, he learned that neither would last out the hour. Still, he made them as comfortable as he could.

Pashipaho sat with head hung low, his eyes closed. Tears streaked Rebecca's face as she tenderly stroked his hands.

"We should go," Davy announced. Where there were a few Sauks, there might be a lot more. Or maybe the Atsinas had heard the ruckus.

The warrior stirred, bloodshot eyes centered on Davy. "Why did you come after us, white man? What are we to you?"

"You're people, just like me," Davy said. "I heard Rebecca scream and came to help. Anyone would have done the same."

"No. Not everyone."

"Come back with me," Davy said. "We'll divvy up our weapons and give you what we can spare. My pard has a blanket he'll likely part with if Rebecca flutters her eyelashes." Shouldering the rifle, he walked past them and did not turn to see if they followed. The decision was theirs.

Footsteps verified that the pair were behind him. Davy gauged how safe it was by the chirping of the birds and the chattering the squirrels. No one else was abroad.

After hiking a quarter of a mile to the stream, Davy hunkered to splash water on his face and neck and treat himself to a drink. The Sauk lay flat next to him and dipped his entire head under the water.

A flat rock enticed Rebecca to sit and drink daintily by cupping her palm. She observed her reflection and bent lower. "Oh, my," she said. "I look a sight." Lacking a comb, she made do with her fingers, then smoothed her clothes.

Davy hiked his shirt to dab water on the knife wound. The blade had creased him, no more, but it stung constantly.

Rebecca gazed thoughtfully into the distance. "I've sure made a mess of my life, haven't I?" she mused aloud. "And all I ever wanted was to live in peace with the man I care for." She swiveled her head. "We overheard my uncle, Mr. Crockett. That's why we cut out. We were afraid you'd do what he wanted and shoot Pashipaho."

"My ears for a heel tap if I ever let someone talk me into going against my grain," Davy said. "I'm no man's lapdog." He lowered the shirt. "As for the other, there's no denying that your life is in a hellacious knot. But it's been my experience that most knots can be unraveled if a body has the patience and the perseverance."

Rebecca smiled wanly. "There you go again. You're a regular fount of wisdom. Mighty rare for someone who is half horse and half gator."

Davy chortled. "Folks in my neck of the woods like to boast almost as much as they like their horns of liquor. Why, at election time, we wear down most of the stumps in the county telling tales that would make a gypsy blush." Standing, he added self-consciously, "I reckon it's in my blood."

Their conversation had relaxed Rebecca. She hummed as she rose to go. Not so Pashipaho. Wearing a grim mask, he brought up the rear.

Davy could hardly wait to rejoin Flavius and be on

their way. The delay was keeping them from hearth and home, and his powerful hankering to see his wife and sprouts had grown more powerful thanks to Rebecca and the Sauk.

Their predicament reminded Davy of his courting days, back when he had sparked his first wife, Polly Finley. Just when they thought their nuptials were sewn up, after he had made arrangements with a parson and was all set to tie the knot, her mother had risen in righteous resistance and denied permission. Eventually, the marriage had taken place, but for a while there, he had been as worried as a fox in coon kennel that it would fall through.

Being opposed by a flighty prospective mother-in-law in no way compared to the ordeal Rebecca and Pashipaho had suffered. But it gave him a different perspective than most. He could sympathize with their plight. Which was why he had gone out of his way to help.

Davy saw the campsite. Flavius sat with his back to the stump, body sagging, apparently enjoying a nap. Davy grinned—until he realized Norval was missing. "What in the world?" he exclaimed, and moved into the middle of the clearing. Too late, he spied the shadowy shapes lurking along the fringe of the vegetation. Too late, he tried to bring up his rifle.

"Do it and you die!" snarled one of those shapes, as into the sunlight strode Norval, Cyrus, and John Kayne.

Chapter Eleven

For a heartbeat the tableau was frozen in time and place. Then Rebecca Worthington flung a hand to her bosom and backed up, shouting, "Run, my love! It's a trap!"

Instead of fleeing by himself, however, Pashipaho leaped forward, snagged her wrist, and spun with her. It was a grand but futile gesture. Futile, in that Norval moved between them and the trees and trained a cocked pistol on the Sauk.

"You're not going anywhere, Injun," the settler said. "We've got plans for you."

Davy was helpless to intervene. Cyrus had him covered. One twitch and he'd be shot, if the mad gleam in Cyrus's beady eyes was any indication.

John Kayne came over. Acting discomfited by what he had to do, he said, "I'm real sorry about this, friend," and stripped Davy of weapons. "But I can't risk having you do something we'll both regret. I've no desire to make wolf meat of you."

"Speak for yourself," Cyrus growled, extending his pistol. "Were it up to me, I'd as soon blow his stinkin' brains out or gut him for the buzzards to finish off."

Kayne turned, the muzzle of his rifle ending up a hand's width from the hothead's abdomen. "I've warned you once. I won't waste my breath again. He's given us no call to rub him out."

Cyrus snorted. "I don't cotton to meddlers," he said, as if that were justification enough to kill someone.

"We can't fault a man for doing what he thinks is right," Kayne said. "Besides, he fought by our side up on that hill. I saw him kill one of the heathens with my own eyes." Moving a safe distance, Kayne deposited Davy's arms on the grass. "We'll stick to the plan, Cy. That's final."

Rebecca had slid around Pashipaho to shield him with her own body from Norval's pistol. "What plan were you talking about, Uncle?" she demanded apprehensively.

It was Cyrus who answered, venom lacing each syllable. "We've decided to make an example of your red bastard, girl. We're takin' him back with us and holdin' a trial, all legal-like. And then we're going to hang the son of a bitch, just as legal-like."

Norval nodded. "It'll show the Sauks that our law applies to their kind as well as ours, and it'll teach them not to rise up against their betters."

A brittle laugh rattled from Cyrus. "Folks will come from miles around to see the scum's neck stretched. We'll make a holiday of it, with a picnic and a church social and all. Everyone will have a fine time."

Rebecca pressed back against Pashipaho. "Dear Lord, no! I won't let you hurt him!"

"Let us?" Cyrus said, and guffawed. "Sugarplum,

there ain't a damn thing you can do to stop us."

Davy had noticed that despite the loud voices and the commotion, Flavius had not moved. "What did you do to my pard?" he asked.

John Kayne motioned, implicitly giving permission for Davy to go to the stump. "I'm afraid that I had to rap him on the noggin with a limb. But I didn't use my full strength. He should come around shortly."

Flavius was breathing evenly. His pulse was normal. Davy ran a hand over his friend's head, finding a bump the size of a walnut. Going to the stream, he filled his coonskin cap. As the cold water trickled down over Flavius's face, Harris groaned, then coughed, then revived, sitting bolt upright.

"What the hell?"

"Relax. You're still in the land of the living." Davy stopped pouring and emptied out the rest.

Pain pounded dully between Flavius's ears. Wincing, he slowly rose high enough to sit on the stump. He did not need to ask what had happened. The last he remembered was hearing a stealthy footfall behind him, and starting to pivot. "If we ever make it home to Tennessee," he muttered, "I swear to high heaven that I'm never leaving Matilda again. I've learned my lesson."

Cyrus tittered. "Too bad others ain't as smart as you, fat man. We'd all have been saved a heap of grief if my bride-to-be knew her proper place."

"Damn you!" Rebecca railed. "I don't care what my father wants. Drag me back, if you will, but I'll never marry you. I'll shoot myself first."

"You say that now," Cyrus said. "But in a few months you'll have forgotten all about this Injun. In a year, you'll leap at the chance to be my wife. Any gal would."

Blood Hunt

The settlers wasted no more time. Pashipaho was bound, and none too gently. When Rebecca objected to how hard Cyrus was tying the knots, Cyrus bound her, as well. She and the Sauk were swung onto the horses. With Cyrus leading the sorrel and Kayne the bay, their little group wended their way southward.

Davy and Flavius trailed the horses and were in turn followed by Norval, whose cocked pistol was rock-steady. A strip torn from his shirt served as a bandage.

Depressed by the turn of events, Flavius hiked morosely along. He had looked forward to being shed of the woman and the warrior. Now they were no better off than they had been earlier—worse even, since it might be days before they were allowed to resume their journey.

Davy plodded glumly, too, more for show than anything else. Giving up was as foreign to him as the Greek alphabet. He wanted to dupe Norval into believing he had resigned himself to his fate, though, so Norval would lower that pistol and he could turn the tables.

The afternoon sun blazed a tedious arc. Davy plucked the end off a blade of grass and chewed on it to moisten his mouth. He did not waste his energy trying to persuade Cyrus to be lenient with Pashipaho. Hatred fed on bloodshed, and Cyrus was hate incarnate.

Out of the woodland hove the hill. John Kayne gave it a wide berth and slowed so drastically that Cyrus complained. "Have you forgotten so soon, boy?" Kayne responded. "He-Bear and his savage ilk are roaming these parts, seeking our scalps. And I'm partial to mine, thank you."

As usual, Cyrus scoffed. "Hell, those vermin are hightailin' it back to whatever pit spawned them with

143

their tails between their legs."

"They licked us, as I recollect," Kayne said dryly.

"Through no fault of ours," Cyrus said. "Some of the connivin' devils were hidin' in the weeds. They didn't fight fair."

Davy could not resist. "And you did? With those men you had up in the trees?"

"That was a precaution, nothin' more. When dealin' with rabid wolves, anything goes."

Some men, Davy reflected, made a habit of bending and twisting the truth to suit their own fancy. For Cyrus to brand the Atsinas as rabid was an injustice to the Atsinas. But when it came to being ruthless, few could hold a candle to the impending groom.

Davy stretched to relieve stiffness in his back. In doing so, he caught a furtive glance that Pashipaho gave John Kayne and Cyrus. The Sauk was up to something. He saw Pashipaho look at Rebecca, saw the slight bob of her chin.

They were going to make a break for it. Davy would do what he could, even at the cost of taking a bullet. He tried to catch Flavius's eye, but Flavius walked as one en route to the gallows, with head low and features downcast. To distract the settlers, Davy cleared his throat and said, "You know, I've had runs of bad luck before, but this beats all. Reminds me of the time I was bear hunting. My dogs sniffed one out, and it lit out like its paws were on fire. When I caught up to them, that old bear was skinning up a huge tree. I took a bead, but he dropped quick as a snake into a hole."

"Who cares?" Cyrus said.

"I haven't gotten to the point yet," Davy said. Out of the corner of an eye he glimpsed Pashipaho grip the sorrel's mane. "For no sooner did that bear van-

144

ish inside the trunk of that tree than the most god-awful roaring and rumbling came out of the hole. And the next second, so did the bear, with an even bigger bear nipping at its hindquarters."

"How interestin'," Cyrus commented sarcastically.

"What's your point?" Norval asked.

"My point is that bears and people have more in common than you'd think. We ought to never go poking our noses into someone else's private space."

Cyrus looked back at him. "Strange talk comin' from a meddler like you, Tennessee."

Suddenly Pashipaho whooped and slapped his legs against the bay's sides. The horse exploded, hurtling into John Kayne and sending him sprawling. Guiding the horse with his legs alone, Pashipaho sped toward the undergrowth.

Rebecca tried to follow him. She kicked and prodded, but Cyrus held on to the sorrel's reins with both hands. The sorrel trotted a few yards and stopped.

"Stop, you!" Norval bellowed, scampering to the left to get a clear shot. "Come back here or I'll shoot!"

Pashipaho could have made it anyway. He was so close to cover that in another few bounds he would have been lost among the trees. But on seeing that Rebecca had been caught, he straightened and called out, "I will do as you say! Do not fire!"

"No!" Rebecca urged. "Keep going! I'll be fine! You matter more!"

The Sauk would not listen. Swinging the horse around, he meekly brought it to a halt next to John Kayne, who had risen. Kayne grasped the reins without comment and did not retaliate.

Cyrus did not share the tall frontiersman's forgiving mood. Stomping to the bay, he hooked his left hand into Pashipaho's shirt and heaved, upending the Sauk. Pashipaho hit on his shoulder and attempted to get up, but Cyrus was on him in a whirl-wind of maddened blows, battering him relentlessly on his head and shoulders. Under the onslaught, the warrior crumbled.

"Stop, damn you!" Rebecca raged. She slid off the sorrel, and was seized by her uncle.

Davy took a step, but the business end of Kayne's rifle prevented him from taking another. He had to stand there and watch as Pashipaho was pounded and kicked and smashed with the rifle's stock.

Cyrus did not relent until he was flushed and out of breath. "Try that again and there'll be hell to pay," he rasped, wiping blood off the barrel with a sleeve.

Pashipaho took a long time to stir. Blood seeped from his split forehead, and one ear had been pulped. His turban had fallen off. Cracked knuckles sought purchase on the earth as he pushed to his knees.

Someone groaned, but not the Sauk. Rebecca smacked a heel against Norval's shins. He released her. She darted to the warrior, braced him up, and was brutally shoved by Cyrus.

"Look at you, girl! Makin' a spectacle of yourself! If the good people of Peoria could see you now, they'd want nothin' to do with you."

Boiling with indignation, Rebecca said, "Didn't it ever occur to you, Cy, that maybe I don't care what they want? That I'd be perfectly content if they, and *you*, would all just drop dead?"

Cy raised a hand to strike her but was foiled when Norval scampered between them "Don't you dare lay a finger on her," he warned, the pistol now centered on her suitor. "The poor child is mistreated enough by her own father."

"You heard her!" Cyrus snapped. "No wonder her pa slaps her around if she won't clamp a lid on that tongue of hers." Chest swelling, he bragged, "No wife of mine will ever have loose lips, I can tell you! Once we're hitched, I'll see that she shows some respect."

"I'll never marry you!" Rebecca said.

"Oh?" Chuckling, Cy walked to the bay. "After everyone hears what you've done, no other man but me would want to be your husband. We're destined to be together." To Pashipaho he said, "This time I'm leadin' your horse. And I won't think twice if you act up."

The warrior had to be helped on. Rebecca lingered, tenderly caressing his split cheek.

"Come, girl," Norval said, prying her away.

Rebecca jerked free. "Don't touch me ever again, Uncle. I used to think that you were special, but now I know you're no better than Cy and his breed."

Davy and Flavius trudged elbow to elbow. "I reckon this is another fine fix I've gotten us into," the Irishman confessed.

"If it ain't chickens, it's feathers," Flavius said, and mustered a grin. "You do have a knack, though. Some men were born to be great painters. Some are wizards at music. You just happen to have a talent for attracting trouble like manure attracts flies."

"Lucky me," Davy joked.

Soon the raucous chattering of a squirrel arrested Davy's interest. It was in a tree about seventy yards to their rear, yet it had not uttered a peep when they went by. Hopping from limb to limb, the animal vented its spleen on something in the brush below.

Davy did not attach much importance to the tirade until a flock of sparrows took frenzied wing to the northeast, approximately sixty yards distant. Whatever was out there was drawing closer. "Kayne!" he whispered.

The tall frontiersman gave the sorrel's reins to

Norval and waited for Davy and Flavius to catch up. "What's the matter?"

"Didn't you hear that squirrel?"

Kayne scanned the forest. "No. I've been mulling over what we're doing." His hawkish features were a study in inner torment. "Just between you and me, Crockett, I'm beginning to have my doubts."

"About time," Davy said.

"Who am I to deny Rebecca happiness? Just because I don't think it's right, should I be a party to hanging the man she loves? I'll admit I look down my nose at his kind, but having him for a husband beats leading apes in hell."

The figure of speech was not new to Davy. It alluded to women who died unwed, and stemmed from the general low esteem in which spinsters were held.

A squawking blue jay flapped skyward from a thicket forty-five yards to the north. Davy and Kayne both slowed, Kayne saying softly, "When will I learn? I shouldn't have let my mind wander."

"Warn the others," Davy suggested. "And give us rifles. Empty-handed we can't help much."

Kayne hastened to Norval, whispered in his ear, and passed on to Cyrus, who thoughtlessly brought their small caravan to a stop and announced loudly, "Injuns? Are you sure?"

Flavius swallowed hard. They should have kept going and not let on that they knew they were being shadowed. He was not a violent man, and he had never been given to holding grudges, but it would please him immensely to punch Cyrus full in the mouth.

Davy spotted rustling grass thirty yards off. Elsewhere, a sapling shook. At still another point, weeds bent. Yet the wind had died. So there was more than one. Whether they were Sauks or Atsinas was irrelevant. Either would be out for blood.

Cyrus had let go of the bay and was walking back. "Maybe the Tennesseans are trying to trick us," he said to John Kayne. "I'm not about to hand them a gun until I know for a fact that hostiles are out there."

Out of thin air whizzed an arrow. The shaft thudded into Cyrus's left shoulder, transfixing him and jolting him backward. In sheer reflex he banged off a wild shot, then turned and staggered toward the horses.

More arrows buzzed like riled hornets. Rifles banged, smoke sprouting to pinpoint the shooters. Davy ducked as John Kayne fired, the blast setting his ear to ringing. He skipped backward to grab one of the rifles that had been tied to the sorrel.

A whinny and the sound of a scuffle brought Davy around in a crouch. Flabbergasted, he saw Cyrus yank Rebecca out of the saddle, then hook a foot in a stirrup and clamber on. The next moment, the sorrel was racing southward with Cyrus clinging on for dear life. And with it went the extra rifles and pistols.

A lead ball thudded into the soil next to Flavius. Crabbing to the left, he hollered, "A rifle! Give me a rifle!" Then he saw the fleeing settler. Queasiness overcame him as he realized that they must face the war party unarmed. "Davy? What do we do?"

Davy was asking himself the same question. He scampered toward Rebecca, but Pashipaho beat him to her side by vaulting from the bay, which immediately ran off after the sorrel.

It dawned on Davy that Norval had not entered the fray. Looking, he learned why. The grizzled oldster was on his knees, a lance jutting from his left thigh.

They were being decimated.

Only John Kayne held the warriors at bay. He had fired one pistol and drawn his other one. Slowly retreating, he swung from right to left and back again, seeking a target the elusive Indians were loath to present.

Pashipaho, even with his wrists bound, practically threw Rebecca into the vegetation, then hurtled in after her. Norval, somehow heaving upright, tottered on their heels.

Davy was left in the open, arrows and bullets whisking on either side. "We have to find cover!" he yelled to Flavius, and suited his own actions to his words. Angling into the trees, he ran flat out for over fifty feet, fully expecting his friend to follow him. But when he drew up in a patch of wildflowers, Flavius was nowhere to be seen.

Eager to go find him, Davy started to retrace his steps. A dusky silhouette materialized a dozen yards off. It was a warrior armed with a war club.

The thick foliage kept Davy from seeing whether the man was a Sauk or an Atsina. Lowering onto his stomach, he crawled eastward, applying his weight carefully in order to avoid breaking twigs.

The warrior moved into the open. A raven mane, husky build, and war paint pegged him as a member of He-Bear's band. The Big Belly prowled southward, passing within thirty feet.

What Davy would not have given for a gun! He had a perfect shot and could not take it. Obtaining a weapon was critical. He heard Kayne's second pistol boom, heard the whoops of the Atsinas, two more rifle shots, then the drum of feet speeding to the southwest.

Kayne was seeking to escape. The Atsinas were after him. But not all of them, as furtive movement told Davy. Another warrior was creeping in his general direction, this one holding a rifle with a brass name-plate on the stock.

Davy dug his fingers into the soil and palmed a handful of dirt and grass. The Atsina was gazing intently beyond him. Clearly, the warrior had spotted someone.

Tucking his chin to his chest, Davy shifted just enough to see the area behind him. His blood chilled. He was not given to profanity, as many were by habit and sloth, but he mentally cursed a storm.

Norval Worthington was propped against an oak. Bent in weakness and fatigue, sweat dripping from his glistening brow, he had wrapped both hands around the lance embedded in his thigh and was struggling his utmost to pull it out. Blood soaked the bottom of his leg and his palms. A sob tore from him when the lance moved a fraction.

The Atsina slid nearer, his attention focused on the settler to the exclusion of all else. Stopping, he raised the rifle, but held his fire, opting to get a little closer.

Davy prayed that the warrior would not notice him. Bracing his elbows and knees, he held his breath as the Big Belly came to within ten feet, then eight, then six.

Halting again, the warrior sighted down the barrel while slowly uncoiling. At that range he could not possibly miss.

Come closer! Davy mentally screamed, and when the man didn't, when the Atsina was undeniably about to fire, he heaved up and attacked.

The startled Atsina automatically recoiled. Davy swatted at the rifle at the very split second that it discharged. The black powder flashed. Burning smoke enveloped him, stinging his eyes, shrouding the warrior.

Flailing at the cloud, Davy glided to one side. He

must not give the Atsina time to reload! As he took another step, the warrior reared out of the cloud, gripping his rifle by the barrel.

Davy jerked his arm up as the rifle swept down. Intense agony spiked his arm, his shoulder. Another blow smashed into his ribs. His knees bent as the Atsina towered over him, the man's eyes wide with hatred.

Like a lashing bullwhip, Davy drove himself upward and hurled the dirt into the Atsina's face. The man backed off, blinking rapidly. Tears smeared brown by the dirt trickled from the corners of his eyes.

Davy grabbed the rifle and the warrior grabbed him. Grappling, they staggered against a tree. The Atsina's sturdy legs pumped, slamming Davy against the trunk. The rifle was across his chest, pinning him in place. Grunting, the man wrenched the rifle higher. Cool metal gouged into Davy's neck, choking off his breath and threatening to crush his throat.

Straining, Davy pushed the rifle off him, but only a few inches. The Atsina was uncommonly strong. Davy's muscles bulged, yet he could not move the man any farther. The warrior's snarling visage was so close, drops of spittle sprinkled him when the Atsina unexpectedly threw everything he had into a supreme effort.

The rifle gouged into Davy's throat again. And now, try as he might, Davy could not push it off. He found it first hard to breathe, then impossible. A fraction at a time, the Atsina was accomplishing what none of the Creeks had ever been able to do.

He was killing Davy.

Chapter Twelve

Flavius Harris had heard Davy Crockett yell and saw his friend sprint into the undergrowth. Heaving to his feet, Flavius slanted toward his friend, but as the vegetation closed around him, he tripped over an ankle-high rock hidden by the high grass. Sprawling, he caught himself on his hands and knees.

The thunder of rifles and the whoop of a warrior somewhere close by inspired him to catapult into the woods. Afraid that the warrior was right on his heels, he ran blindly for a score of yards. When he looked back and discovered that no one was after him, he slowed.

The Irishman had disappeared. Worry knifing through him, Flavius turned in a complete circle, then hurried in the direction he thought Davy had been heading. It soon became apparent that it was the wrong direction.

Flavius stopped, hunkered, and listened. Guns

blasted a few more times. Brush crackled at the passage of unseen bodies, followed by silence, an unnerving quiet that raised goose bumps all over him.

Flavius swallowed hard. His best guess was that the unseen ambushers were the Atsinas. According to the settlers, the Sauks did not own many rifles.

As near as Flavius recollected, six Atsinas survived the battle on the hill—six heavily armed warriors, any one of whom possessed more woodcraft than he ever would. What chance did he stand without a weapon?

Casting about, Flavius spied a short broken branch that made a dandy club. Hefting it a few times restored a smidgen of confidence.

Taking a deep breath, Flavius snuck into the trees, moving southward, which he assumed the others would do, provided any of them survived. Furtive movement and disturbing whispers of sound grated on his nerves. He imagined that he was surrounded by the war party, that all six were slinking closer and closer. At any moment now they would pounce.

A commotion directly ahead brought him to a halt. Ducking, he sought the source. Unable to see anyone, he reluctantly advanced, his palms so sweaty on his makeshift club that it nearly slipped from his grasp.

There! Something moved! Flavius darted behind a clump of weeds. When no shots rang out and no lusty war whoops punctured the woodland, he peeked out. An Atsina had someone pinned against a tree, someone whose buckskins looked awfully familiar. It jarred Flavius to realize that the man was Davy.

Forgetting all concern for his own safety, forgetting everything except the welfare of his friend, Flavius ran toward the tree. The two men were so engrossed in their life-and-death struggle that neither saw him until he was on top of them.

The Atsina snarled and pivoted, whipping the rifle in a short arc. But Flavius already had his heavy club at the apex of its own swing. He brought it crashing down on the warrior's head. To his horror, it broke in half on impact, leaving a worthless stub in his hands.

Flavius hurled it from him and cocked his fists to defend himself as best he was able. Inexplicably, the Atsina had not moved—inexplicable until Flavius saw the tremendous gash in the man's head and the mix of blood and gore that oozed from the opening and down over the warrior's painted features.

The Big Belly's eyelids were fluttering, the whites of his eyes showing. He made another effort to employ the rifle, but it slipped from quivering fingers. Stiff-legged, the man took a few shambling steps. His eyes rolled up into his head as he fell to the turf and lay shaking convulsively.

Astonishment riveted Flavius. He looked at his own hands, amazed at his power. Now he knew how Samson must have felt.

A groan brought Flavius back to the world of reality. Davy had slumped and was sucking in air. Clasping him, Flavius said softly, "It's all right, pard. I took care of him."

Davy had seen as much. He wanted to thank Flavius, but he was too weak to speak. Rarely had he been so close to death's door. Another few moments and his soul would have taken flight. His throat hurt abominably. Each swallow was torture. He rested, gathering his energy.

The crack of a tree limb many yards off prompted Flavius to help himself to the Atsina's rifle and to strip off the man's ammo pouch and powder horn.

An added bonus was a Green River knife in a beaded sheath. He commenced reloading.

Davy watched for more warriors. It felt as if sand coated his throat; breathing was still painful. Rubbing his neck and tilting his head back helped relieve some of the pain, but not enough.

"What do we do next?" Flavius whispered. "I vote we go after our horses. None of those mangy settlers give a damn about us, so why should we care what happens to them?"

The query reminded Davy of Norval Worthington, and he turned.

Rebecca's uncle was flat on his back, his right leg bent unnaturally, his left leg propped up by the lance that still impaled the limb. Norval attempted to rise, but fell back again with an anguished moan.

Davy forced his legs to function. He staggered over and knelt. He assumed that blood loss from the thigh wound accounted for Norval's condition, but a bullet hole on the left side of the settler's chest was to blame. The wild shot that the Atsina got off had hit home, after all.

Norval's eyes flitted wildly. "Who's there?" he croaked. "I can't see!"

"It's Crockett," Davy answered, taking the man's hand.

Sighing, Norval said, "I'm hit bad, ain't I?"

"Yes."

"Damn." Norval was silent a bit, his jaw muscles twitching. "Never figured on buying the farm for a while yet," he commented. "I reckon it doesn't do to try and second-guess the Almighty."

Flavius joined them. The man's plight did not arouse much sympathy in him, not after the shoddy treatment he'd suffered at his hands. In his estimation, none of this would have happened, no one would have died, if the settlers had left well enough alone.

"Is that your friend?" Norval asked. When Davy confirmed that it was, Norval spoke in a rush. "I can feel myself slipping away. I don't have much time left before I'm called to my reward, so please listen." His grip on Davy's hand tightened. "I need the two of you to make me a promise, so I can die content."

"What kind of promise?" Davy inquired, suspecting what it would be.

"Give me your solemn word that you'll stop my niece from taking up with that stinking heathen. Pledge to me that you'll kill him."

Flavius was offended by the man's unmitigated gall. "No," he said flatly. "As she keeps telling everyone, she's a grown woman. She can do as she pleases."

"What about you, Crockett?" Norval said. "Surely you're wise enough to see that it would be the biggest mistake of her life?"

"It's hers to make."

Norval was breathing raggedly, but that did not stop him from digging his nails into Davy's arm and partially pulling himself up. "Please! Don't let me die knowing she'll disgrace the family name." Tears gushed, dampening his cheeks. "I'm begging you! Do you hear? *Begging* you!"

"No," Davy said.

Groaning, Norval sank back down. "Damn you," he whimpered, then declared forcefully, "I curse you both! May your lives be filled with misery! May you meet violent, awful ends! It's the least you deserve for your betrayal of your own race!"

"Norval—" Davy began softly.

"I don't want to hear it!" the settler said much too loudly. "You're scum! I wish to hell some of the boys from Peoria were here, and not the two of you!"

"Ask us to promise anything else," Davy offered.

"No!" Norval fumed, shaking his fist. "If I could see, I'd teach you! I'd—" His mouth widened, his eyes narrowed, and his fist plopped between them. "I'd—" he said again. It was the last sound he was to make other than the thump of his head striking the ground.

Davy did not dally. Somewhere or other Norval had dropped his rifle, but a pair of polished flintlocks were tucked under the man's belt. Davy appropriated them, as well as a pouch and horn. His own tomahawk was nestled at the small of Norval's back, and Davy patted it as he added it to his waist arsenal.

Flavius had heard indistinct noises to the south, among them the nicker of a horse. "That way?" he said.

"Need you ask?" Davy took the lead, a smoothbore pistol in each hand. Now that he was armed, he strode quickly, boldly, his ire at the Atsinas matched by his anxiety for Rebecca.

Flavius wondered why his friend had thrown caution to the wind. One look at Davy's face was ample explanation. He had seen that look before, during the Creek War, right before a battle, and again when a man had accused Davy of being a liar. The Irishman had his dander up. Crockett was infernal mad, as the canebrake folk phrased it, and woe betide anyone who dared oppose him.

The whinnies of the horse were a beacon. Davy's sense of self-preservation tempered his anger when he spotted the two animals in a clearing; he slowed to a snail's pace.

Flavius was as jittery as a fly caught in a spider's web. He would have dearly loved to take wing and get out of there, but he could never forsake his companion. It mystified him that the sorrel and bay had been left unattended. By rights, Cyrus should be half-way to Peoria.

Davy drew up at some brambles. The reins to both animals had been left dangling. The sorrel was doing all the nickering, ears pricked, nostrils flared, its attention on a stately willow. Or, rather, on what was taking place *under* the willow. Figures moved. Someone cried out.

Davy circled from the east where the cover was better. Two Atsinas were under the tree, bent over someone, brandishing knives.

Flavius could not quite figure out what was going on until one of the blades dipped and scarlet drops flew. The man on the ground screamed, but it was stifled by a hand over his mouth. On recognizing who it was, Flavius was disinclined to interfere.

Cyrus had not gotten very far. His clothes had been sliced from his body and he lay as naked as a jaybird, held down by the weight of the warriors on his arms and legs. His chest was crisscrossed with crimson lines where their knives had been busy. From a small cut in his throat leaked more blood.

The worst was Cyrus's groin. From that day on, Flavius would shudder whenever he recalled the atrocity. Mutilation had that effect.

Davy motioned for Flavius to stay put and slid ten paces to the left. The Big Bellies never looked up from their grisly handiwork. Cyrus quaked with each slash, his struggles intensifying to no avail.

The larger of the Atsinas pressed the tip of his knife against the hothead's belly. A feral grin hinted at his foul purpose.

Of all the inhuman deeds humankind perpetrated, Davy rated coldhearted butchery as the vilest. He could not stand to see it inflicted, not even to someone as deserving of torment as Cyrus. In three bounds he was under the tree, the pistol in his right hand centered on the large warrior.

The Atsina glanced up. Where others might have dived flat or fled outright, he growled like a beast at bay and sprang, the blade smeared with Cyrus's blood thirsting for Davy's.

A stroke of the trigger, and a lead ball smashed into the man's sternum with the force of a battering ram. Spun completely around, the warrior sagged but did not fall.

At the same instant, the second Atsina bellowed and leaped up. Rather than get close enough to use his knife, he snapped his arm back to throw it.

Flavius had the man dead to rights. His sights aligned, he fired at the warrior's left ear. The Atsina was kicked sideways, tripped over Cyrus, and landed lifeless, two ear canals where there should have been one.

Davy took a step, but the large Atsina turned. The warrior's knife arm flicked out, dipping lower as the man who held the weapon keeled over. Knife and owner smacked the earth in front of him.

Cyrus was trembling uncontrollably, as if he were freezing to death. Teeth chattering, he mewed like a stricken kitten. "Help me! For God's sake, help me!"

Flavius fought down bile. There was little anyone could do, short of a parson. "I'm sorry for you," he said, and was surprised at his sincerity.

Propping an elbow, Cyrus raised himself high enough to glimpse the lower half of his body. Gulping, he blanched and broke into choking sobs. "No, no, no, no, no, no! Please tell me it ain't so!"

"We can take you to the settlement," Davy proposed while surveying the vegetation that fringed the willow. Three of the Atsinas had been accounted for, leaving He-Bear and two others to wreak havoc.

Whining, Cyrus closed his eyes and shook his head.

"I'll fetch a blanket to cover you."

"A gun."

"What?"

"Find my pistol. One of the savages took it."

Davy balked at the request. His parents had instilled into him the belief that where there was life, there was hope. No one should ever give up, no matter how terrible their affliction.

"For the love of God, my pistol!" Cyrus repeated. "Please! I hurt so bad!"

Ever after, Davy would ponder what he would have done if Flavius had not taken the matter out of his hands by going to where the pistol lay and bringing it back.

Wordlessly, Flavius gave the flintlock to Cyrus. He did not care to stay and witness the outcome, but he paused when Cyrus blinked up at them.

"I'm obliged, fellers. You're decent, after all. Sorry for the aggravation we caused."

"Is there a doctor in the settlement?" Davy asked. It wasn't too late, he told himself. They could staunch the flow of blood and rig up a travois.

Cyrus did not seem to hear. "Tell that fool girl she got her wish. Should tickle her." A low chuckle gurgled from his red-flecked lips. "You want to hear the funny part? I never was partial to Rebecca. Marrying her was my pa's idea. How he carried on! You'd think he wanted her for himself." Resting the pistol on his bloody chest, he gazed thoughtfully into the willow branches.

Flavius thought that possibly the man had changed his mind. "Rest easy. We'll do what we can."

"The rotten bitch!" Cyrus declared out of the blue.

Then he cocked the flintlock, shoved the muzzle into his mouth, and squeezed the trigger.

Davy jumped as the ball burst out the top of the fiancé's head. Davy experienced no remorse, no regrets. Ripping out a handful of grass, he wiped his pants. "Get the horses before they wander off."

Grateful to be doing anything other than staring at the bloody corpse, Flavius collected both animals. The prospect of heading home at long last thrilled him. "Let's light a shuck while we can," he urged.

"You're forgetting something," Davy said.

No, Flavius was not. "Let them get by on their own," he responded. "We don't owe any of them."

"We owe ourselves." To forestall debate, Davy swung onto the sorrel. "You go east, after Rebecca and Pashipaho. I'll go southwest after Kayne. I think the rest of the Atsinas went after him."

"You *think*?"

"Keep your eyes skinned." Not waiting to see if Flavius complied, Davy applied his heels. Being on top of the horse, he could see a lot farther. So long as he avoided heavy growth, the Big Bellies would be hard-pressed to take him by surprise.

Looping wide, Davy soon found tracks. Since John Kayne wore moccasins he made himself, distinguishing them from the three sets of Atsina prints was easy. Kayne's lengthy stride showed he had been running flat out. In contrast, the warriors had been pacing themselves, counting on their quarry to tire before they did.

Davy brought his mount to a trot. The four men did not have much of a lead, so he should catch them soon.

After the stillness brought on by the gunshot, the pounding of the sorrel's hooves seemed unusually loud. The forest tapered, the leafy carpet replaced by grass. A wide gully barred his path, flanked on the right by a hill. At the brink he reined up to determine how steep the walls were.

Up out of the shadowy bottom rushed a trio of bronzed demons, shrieking like banshees. Foremost was He-Bear, bearing Davy's rifle. The Atsina chief brought it to his shoulder to shoot.

Davy was a shade faster. Extending the pistol in his right hand, he cocked it and squeezed. Nothing happened. The hammer clicked dry. For a second he thought that it had been a misfire.

But it was worse than that. He had committed the cardinal mistake any frontiersman could make. What with Cyrus's suicide, and his urgent ride to help Kayne, he had forgotten to reload the pistol after he had shot the Atsina under the willow. Dropping it, Davy clawed at the other flintlock under his belt. He never got it out.

He-Bear had been on the verge of firing when the pistol clicked. Realizing in a twinkling what it meant, he barked commands in his own tongue as a sadistic grin spread over his cruel visage.

The other two warriors leaped. One caught hold of Davy's right arm, the other his left leg. Davy hauled on the reins for the sorrel to back up. The horse tried, nickering and kicking.

Davy worked to free his leg. Suddenly the world turned upside down. Crashing down, he had the breath knocked out of him. Although stunned, he fumbled for the pistol. It was gone.

His arms were viciously wrenched outward. Feet slammed onto his wrists. Pinned, Davy looked up at the two smirking Atsinas.

He-Bear walked into view. To emphasize his intention, he slowly drew his knife and held it so the polished blade mirrored the sunlight. "Other one get away. Now we have you. Good trade, eh, white dog?"

Davy read his doom in the Atsina's merciless eyes. He-Bear leaned toward him, waving the knife in small circles. At any moment Davy expected the blade to plunge into his body. Then a strange thing occurred.

One of the warriors said something. He-Bear and the other Atsina looked up, toward the hill. Utter consternation struck them like a thunderclap. All three stiffened and brought their rifles to bear. The warrior on the right whispered excitedly. The man on the left took his foot off of Davy's arm and began to back off.

Davy made a break for it. Sitting up, he pushed the warrior still standing on his right wrist and raised both arms to ward off the blows sure to descend. Only, none did. The Big Bellies had not taken their eyes off the hill.

Curiosity got the better of him. Davy twisted, and was as dumbstruck as the warriors. From the high grass covering the slope had sprouted dark four-legged forms, more wolves than he had ever beheld in any one place at any one time.

Near the bottom stood an enormous male with a silver-tipped coat. The tip of its left ear was missing.

"It can't be!" Davy blurted.

The sound of his voice broke He-Bear's spell. Scowling, the scarred Atsina brought the rifle muzzle down. Davy lunged, grabbing it and shoving it away from him with one hand as his other swung the tomahawk out and around and sheered it into He-Bear's stomach.

Roaring, the Big Belly lumbered backward. In his left hand was his knife, which he swiped at Davy's face.

Davy ducked. The blade snatched at his coonskin

hat; he propelled himself upward. His tomahawk crossed in front of the knife as the knife reversed direction. He-Bear's left eyebrow and forehead folded in on themselves, a geyser spurted, and the Atsina collapsed like a broken toy.

Davy turned to confront the other two, brandishing his tomahawk, but neither was even looking at him. They were in full flight, making for the sanctuary of the forest. Looking behind him, he was tempted to follow their example.

The wolf pack had come down the hill and was moving toward him. In the lead trotted the enormous male. It padded to within a yard, lingered to sniff and whine, then went on past. The rest of the wolves spread out and filed on by.

Few deigned to notice him. Davy could have reached out and touched some of them, but he refrained. When the last creature melted into the trees, he shook his head and heard his sentiments echoed.

"If I hadn't've seen that with my own eyes, Crockett, I would never believe it. You must live a charmed life."

Across the gully stood John Kayne. He glanced at He-Bear. "I saw the Indians jump you and came as quick as I could."

"I reckon we don't need to worry about the Atsinas anymore," Davy commented.

Kayne scratched his chin. "I ain't never seen the like. I thought that big silver wolf looked a lot like a cub saved from a trap by a hunter named Old Jake, years ago. But it couldn't be. It's been too long."

North of them a rider appeared. Flavius, leading the sorrel, approached at a gallop. "I caught your horse heading for Canada. What happened?"

Davy had a more important question. "Where are Rebecca and Pashipaho?"

"I couldn't find any sign of them. The Sauk covered their tracks real well," Flavius said. He didn't add that he had not searched very hard. "Do we keep hunting?"

"No, we don't," Davy said, and nodded at John Kayne. "How about you?"

The tall frontiersman cradled his rifle in the crook of an arm. "As far as I'm concerned, it's over. Those two can roam free with the wolves, for all I care."

For the first time in a long time, Davy Crockett smiled.

CHEYENNE

JUDD COLE

Don't miss the adventures of Touch the Sky, as he searches for a world he can call his own.

Cheyenne #14: Death Camp. When his tribe is threatened by an outbreak of deadly disease, Touch the Sky must race against time and murderous foes. But soon, he realizes he must either forsake his heritage and trust white man's medicine—or prove his loyalty even as he watches his people die.
___3800-5 $3.99 US/$4.99 CAN

Cheyenne #15: Renegade Nation. When Touch the Sky's enemies join forces against all his people—both Indian and white—they test his warrior and shaman skills to the limit. If the fearless brave isn't strong enough, he will be powerless to stop the utter annihilation of the two worlds he loves.
___3891-9 $3.99 US/$4.99 CAN

WHITE APACHE

Jake
McMasters

Follow Clay Taggart as he hunts the murdering S.O.B.s who left him for dead—and sends them to hell!

#1: Hangman's Knot. Strung up and left to die, Taggart is seconds away from death when he is cut down by a ragtag band of Apaches. Disappointed to find Taggart alive, the warriors debate whether to kill him immediately or to ransom him off. They are hungry enough to eat him, but they think he might be worth more on the hoof. He is. Soon the white desperado and the desperate Apaches form an alliance that will turn the Arizona desert red with blood.

_3535-9 $3.99 US/$4.99 CAN

#2: Warpath. Twelve S.O.B.s were the only reason Taggart had for living. Together with the desperate Apache warriors who'd saved him from death, he'd have his revenge. One by one, he'd hunt the yellowbellies down. One by one, he'd make them wish they'd never drawn a breath. One by one, he'd leave their guts and bones scorching under the brutal desert sun.

_3575-8 $3.99 US/$4.99 CAN

Dorchester Publishing Co., Inc.
65 Commerce Road
Stamford, CT 06902

Please add $1.75 for shipping and handling for the first book and $.50 for each book thereafter. NY, NYC, PA and CT residents, please add appropriate sales tax. No cash, stamps, or C.O.D.s. All orders shipped within 6 weeks via postal service book rate. Canadian orders require $2.00 extra postage and must be paid in U.S. dollars through a U.S. banking facility.

Name_____

Address_____

City _____ State _____ Zip _____

I have enclosed $_____in payment for the checked book(s).

Payment <u>must</u> accompany all orders.☐ Please send a free catalog.

Jake McMasters

**Follow the action-packed adventures of
Clay Taggart, as he fights for revenge against
settlers, soldiers, and savages.**

#7: *Blood Bounty*. The settlers believe Clay Taggart is a
ruthless desperado with neither conscience nor soul. But
Taggart is just an innocent man who has a price on his head.
With a motley band of Apaches, he roams the vast Southwest,
waiting for the day he can clear his name—or his luck runs
out and his scalp is traded for gold.
___3790-4 $3.99 US/$4.99 CAN

#8: *The Trackers*. In the blazing Arizona desert, a wanted
man can end up as food for the buzzards. But since Clay
Taggart doesn't live like a coward, he and his band of
renegade Indians spend many a day feeding ruthless
bushwhackers to the wolves. Then a bloodthirsty trio comes
after the White Apache and his gang. But try as they might
to run Taggart to the ground, he will never let anyone kill
him like a dog.
___3830-7 $3.99 US/$4.99 CAN

Dorchester Publishing Co., Inc.
65 Commerce Road
Stamford, CT 06902

Please add $1.75 for shipping and handling for the first book and
$.50 for each book thereafter. NY, NYC, PA and CT residents,
please add appropriate sales tax. No cash, stamps, or C.O.D.s. All
orders shipped within 6 weeks via postal service book rate.
Canadian orders require $2.00 extra postage and must be paid in
U.S. dollars through a U.S. banking facility.

Name _____
Address _____
City _____ State _____ Zip _____
I have enclosed $_____ in payment for the checked book(s).
Payment <u>must</u> accompany all orders.☐ Please send a free catalog.

TWICE THE FRONTIER ACTION AND ADVENTURE IN ONE GIANT EDITION!

GIANT SPECIAL EDITION:

THE TRAIL WEST
David Thompson

Far from the teeming streets of civilization, rugged pioneers dare to carve a life out of the savage frontier, but few have a prayer of surviving there. Bravest among the frontiersmen is Nathaniel King—loyal friend, master trapper, and grizzly killer. Then a rich Easterner hires Nate to guide him to the virgin lands west of the Rockies, and he finds his life threatened by hostile Indians, greedy backshooters, and renegade settlers. If Nate fails to defeat those vicious enemies, he'll wind up buried beneath six feet of dirt.

_3938-9 $5.99 US/$7.99 CAN

Dorchester Publishing Co., Inc.
65 Commerce Road
Stamford, CT 06902

Please add $1.75 for shipping and handling for the first book and $.50 for each book thereafter. NY, NYC, PA and CT residents, please add appropriate sales tax. No cash, stamps, or C.O.D.s. All orders shipped within 6 weeks via postal service book rate. Canadian orders require $2.00 extra postage and must be paid in U.S. dollars through a U.S. banking facility.

Name_____

Address_____

City _____ State _____ Zip_____

I have enclosed $_____in payment for the checked book(s).

Payment <u>must</u> accompany all orders.☐ Please send a free catalog.

WILDERNESS GIANT SPECIAL EDITION:

PRAIRIE BLOOD
David Thompson

The epic struggle for survival on America's frontier—in a Giant Special Edition!

While America is still a wild land, tough mountain men like Nathaniel King dare to venture into the majestic Rockies. And though he battles endlessly against savage enemies and hostile elements, his reward is a world unfettered by the corruption that grips the cities back east.

Then Nate's young son disappears, and the life he has struggled to build seems worthless. A desperate search is mounted to save Zach before he falls victim to untold perils. If the rugged pioneers are too late—and Zach hasn't learned the skills he needs to survive—all the freedom on the frontier won't save the boy.

_3679-7 $4.99

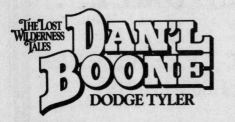